D1560422

A Club in
Montmartre

A Club in
Montmartre

An Encounter with Henri Toulouse-Lautrec

MIKE RESNICK

WATSON-GUPTILL PUBLICATIONS/NEW YORK

Series Editor: Jacqueline Ching
Assistant Editor: Katherine Happ
Production Manager: Joseph Illidge
Book Design: Jennifer Browne

First published in 2005 in the United States by Watson-Guptill Publications,
a division of VNU Business Media, Inc.,
770 Broadway, New York, NY 10003
www.wgpub.com

Library of Congress Cataloging-in-Publication Data

Resnick, Michael D.
A club in Montmartre : an encounter with Henri Toulouse-Lautrec / by Mike Resnick.
p. cm. -- (Art encounters)
Summary: After a beggar girl rescues the drunken, severely deformed French painter Henri
Toulouse-Lautrec, he introduces her to his studio, the nightlife of Montmartre, and the cancan
dancers at the Moulin Rouge club. Includes bibliographical references (p.   ).
ISBN-13: 978-0-8230-0420-1
ISBN-10: 0-8230-0420-1
1. Toulouse-Lautrec, Henri de, 1864-1901--Juvenile fiction. [1. Toulouse-Lautrec, Henri de,
1864-1901--Fiction. 2. Artists--Fiction. 3. Dance--Fiction. 4. Alcoholism--Fiction. 5.
Abnormalities, Human --Fiction. 6. Montmartre (Paris, France)--History--Fiction. 7. Paris
(France)--History--1870-1940--Fiction. 8. France--History--Third Republic, 1870-1940--
Fiction. 9. Moulin-Rouge (Night club : Paris, France)--Fiction.] I. Title. II. Series.
PZ7.R31634Cl 2006 [Fic]--dc22   2006006991

This book was set in Stempel Garamond.

Printed in the U.S.A.

First printing, 2006

1 2 3 4 5 6 7 / 12 11 10 09 08 07 06

To Carol, as always.

*And to the wonderful artists who have painted the covers
of my books:*
Rob Alexander
George Barr
John Berkey
Bob Eggleton
Ed Emshwiller
Kelly Freas
Donato Giancola
Todd Hamilton
David A. Hardy
John Harris
Kevin Johnson
Neil McPheeters
John Picacio
Don Ivan Punchantz
Carol Russo
Barclay Shaw
Darrell K. Sweet

Karel Thole
Boris Vallejo
Darien Vallejo
Michael Whelan
Paul Youll

And while I'm thinking of it, Leonardo da Vinci
and Henri Toulouse-Lautrec

Contents

Preface

Two unique structures in Paris were opened to the public in the year 1889. They were the Eiffel Tower and a nightclub called the Moulin Rouge. I think any reasonable man would have been willing to bet even money that the Moulin Rouge would vanish by the year 1900 and that the Eiffel Tower probably would be replaced with something more impressive long before the year 2000 rolled around.

So much for reasonable men. These two creations have become the universal symbols of Paris—indeed, of France. The Eiffel Tower owes its fame to its size, because it can be seen from just about anywhere in Paris. The Moulin Rouge, on the other hand, owes its fame to one misshapen, alcoholic little man of immense talent, Henri Toulouse-Lautrec.

The son of a wealthy father who was descended from counts and a mother who was an actual countess, young Henri was expected to do great things. Eventually he delivered greater things that anyone could have anticipated—but they were not quite what his parents had in mind. Henri was being trained for a life of wealthy leisure when he broke his thighs. They healed, but his legs stopped growing; and while he had a normal physique from the hips up, he shuffled around on abnormally small legs, never reaching a height of five feet.

His father lost all interest in him. Obviously this was not a son he could show off in public. His mother still doted on him and wanted him to live a life of luxurious seclusion in the family mansion.

Henri had other plans. He had always been interested in art. Now he was determined to prove that his physique would not be a handicap to his work as an artist. He left home and moved to Paris to begin his career. Once there, and feeling himself to be an outcast, he found himself drawn to other outcasts—and there were more outcasts in Montmartre than anywhere else in Paris.

He developed friendships with Edgar Degas, Vincent van Gogh, and a number of other artists; but he belonged to no artistic movement except his own. He was fascinated by the bizarre—circus performers, nightclub performers, prostitutes, all the most colorful denizens of Montmartre—quite possibly because he appeared no more out of the ordinary than any of them. He was accepted almost instantly in Montmartre, and while he took many trips throughout Europe, he always returned there.

Still, while he could pretend that he was no different from anyone else with whom he was associating, all he had to do was look in a mirror to know that he was indeed different; and he turned to drink. He was a confirmed alcoholic in his early twenties, and it was his excessive drinking that eventually killed him at the young age of thirty-six.

Still, drunk or sober, the man was a dedicated artist. My previous book for this series was about Leonardo da Vinci, who lived to a ripe old age; and while some of his work has been lost to posterity, I think it's fair to say that he completed less than twenty paintings in his life-time. Toulouse-Lautrec, despite his early death, completed more than seven hundred paintings, close to three hundred prints, and more than five thousand drawings. Not bad for a man who drank himself into a stupor almost every night.

He was said to have a lively sense of humor, he was of course bet-ter educated than most of the people with whom he associated, and because of his family he never lacked for money. Nonetheless, he never differentiated between commercial work and art for art's sake. In fact, to this day he is considered perhaps the greatest lithographic artist in history, and his two most famous works are his commercial posters of the Moulin Rouge (the subject of this book) and of dancer Jane Avril.

Toulouse-Lautrec was, in his way, a revolutionary—not politically but artistically. He rejected much of what came before him in his art and influenced much of what followed him. Montmartre seems to have had that effect on artists—Toulouse-Lautrec, van Gogh, Degas, Picasso, and many others lived and worked there during a span of twenty years.

I have been to Paris a number of times, and while these days Montmartre looks a lot like New York City's Times Square before Rudi Giuliani cleaned it up, as you walk away from the sleazier clubs and peep shows and into the neighborhood, you begin to get some of the flavor of what it was like in Toulouse-Lautrec's time: endlessly fascinating, and more than a little dangerous.

It was interesting to research this book. I thought I knew a lot about the artist, the Moulin Rouge, and the area; but I kept coming across things I'd never encountered before. The most interesting? The elephant.

(Don't worry. You'll come to it.)

And the more I studied Toulouse-Lautrec, the more complex he became. I wish I'd known him. One thing is certain: drunk or sober, he was never boring.

CHAPTER ONE

A Street in Montmartre

It was three o'clock in the morning, and the odd-looking, bearded little man awkwardly shuffled his way down the boulevard de Clichy, swaying slightly with each step. He held a cane in his left hand but seemed unaware of it and didn't use it to help keep his balance. In his right hand was an open bottle of very expensive cognac, and he took a swallow every few steps.

He was very well dressed and appeared wealthy enough to have hired a horse-drawn carriage. Every now and then he would pass someone on the damp Paris street and offer a greeting or comment, but his words were slurred, and no one could understand what he was saying. It didn't seem to bother anyone; everyone merely smiled at him and moved on, as if this was a normal occurrence.

After a few minutes he stopped and leaned against a building. As they had done when he was walking, the denizens of the Boulevard ignored him, except for the occasional woman who would look at him, shake her head sadly, and then continue on her way.

When he felt capable of walking again, he continued his trek. Then as he came to the junction of the boulevard de Clichy and rue

Frochot, he stared down at the curb. He tentatively moved one foot forward, but pulled it back almost immediately. He spent almost a full minute laboriously switching his cane to his right hand and his bottle to his left, then moved his other foot forward—and again pulled it back. He stood motionless, staring at the curb as if it presented a physical barrier that he was incapable of negotiating.

A girl, barely into her teens, dirt smudging her face and tattered clothes, stood in the shadows of a building on rue Frochot, watching him curiously. Finally she got up the courage to speak to a woman who was walking past.

"That man," she said, "what is the matter with him?"

"Him?" said the woman with a shrug. "He's the painter—Henri something-or-other. He comes here to Pigalle almost every night after all the expensive clubs have closed."

"But why does he just stand there?"

"He's drunk, of course. I don't think I've ever seen him sober."

"There is something different about him," persisted the girl.

"Of course there is," said the woman. "Take a good look at him. He's a freak."

The girl stared at the man through the darkness.

"He's not a freak," she said finally. "But there is something different about him."

"I told you to take a good look. You'll figure it out."

The girl frowned and studied the man again.

"It's his legs," she announced at last. "It's like they were cut off at the knees."

"There are those who say that's exactly what happened to him," replied the woman. "Do you see the curb? It's about six inches above the street where he's standing, and he knows with those shrunken legs of his he'll fall flat on his face if he tries to cross the street." She chuckled. "He could walk fifteen feet to his right and there's almost no curb at all, but he's too drunk to notice."

The girl stared at the man's legs, then saw him start to sway again.

"They'll kill him," she said at last.

"Who will kill who?" asked the woman.

"The men who dwell in the shadows and alleyways of Pigalle," answered the girl. "You can see that he has money, and he's going to pass out at any minute. They'll rob him and cut his throat," she sighed. "It's too bad."

"You're new to Pigalle, aren't you?" said the woman.

"I've been here eight days," said the girl defensively. "Maybe nine."

"Begging?"

The girl lowered her eyes and nodded her head. "Yes. We lived on a farm, but cholera killed my mother and my sister this winter. My father took me to Paris; but one day he didn't come home, and I never saw him again." A tear rolled down her cheek. "I don't know what happened to him. There was no money, so I tried selling flowers."

"I don't see any flowers."

"Two men came by and told me I'd have to pay them before they'd let me sell the flowers. Since I couldn't pay them, I ran away and came to Montmartre; but the same thing happened again with different men. When I couldn't pay, they hit me and took my flowers away."

"There's no need to be ashamed of begging," said the woman. "It's only temporary. For now you'll beg. In another year or two you can move up to what I do. Maybe sooner." She stared at the girl. "What's your name?"

The girl hesitated a moment, then answered. "Dany."

"And I am Fabien. We won't bother with last names. The fewer people in Montmartre who know your real name, the less likely the police are to learn it." She stared at the girl. "When's the last time you had a hot meal, Dany?"

"What day is it?"

"Thursday."

"Monday, I think," said Dany.

"You're a very pretty girl," said Fabien, appraising her with a professional eye. "Or you could be once, you were cleaned up." She nodded toward the artist. "Maybe he will pay you to model for him once he sobers up."

Dany turned her attention back to the artist, who was still tottering on the edge of the curb, and shook her head. "Any minute they will rob him and slit his throat. He looks so helpless with those little legs."

"The regulars won't touch him," said Fabien. "But of course new people are always moving into the area, looking for easy pickings."

"Why won't the regulars touch him?" asked Dany. "After all, he's rich and he's drunk, and he can't run away."

"He's one of us."

"Him?" said Dany disbelievingly.

"Maybe I said it wrong," admitted Fabien. "Let me put it another way. He doesn't just visit Montmartre occasionally to spend his money on the *poules* and the liquor like most of those pigs you see.

He lives here."

"Lots of people who live here get robbed and killed," said Dany. "Even I know that."

"He spends money here almost every night. He buys a woman, he buys drinks, he tips people who help him, sometimes when his legs hurt too much for him to walk back to his studio he rents a room. We all make money off him. If someone robs and kills him, they're robbing *us*—and you know what happens to those who rob the night people of Pigalle."

Dany didn't know, but she could hazard a pretty good guess. After all, it was just a section of Montmartre, and everyone knew about Montmartre.

"So you just let him lie where he falls and hope he can walk home in the morning?" she asked.

"What would you have me do?" demanded Fabien. "Give him my blanket? Carry him up three flights of stairs to my room?"

"No," said Dany, looking back at the man. "I guess not."

The man was still considering how to step down from the curb. Finally he seemed to make up his mind. He leaned forward, placed the tip on his cane on the street, and was about to take a step when the cane slipped on the wet pavement. As it flew out of his hand, he uttered a brief curse, then toppled over.

For a moment Dany thought he was dead, but then he groaned, rolled over onto his belly, and tried to get up. She could see his legs bending, so she knew they had joints and had not been cut off at the knees; but he was either too drunk or too badly injured to climb to his feet. Eventually he saw his cane glistening in a puddle about ten feet away and he tried to crawl to it, but he collapsed again.

Twice more he tried to reach his cane. Finally he rolled over onto his back and lay still. Passersby ignored him, simply walking around him. Bodies in the streets of Pigalle weren't exactly a rarity.

"Well, that's that," said Fabien. "At least he didn't throw up all over himself tonight. I don't know about his paintings, but he himself always puts on a good show." She placed a hand on Dany's shoulder. "Do you see that building over there, the one with the arches over the doorway?"

Dany looked at the run-down building and nodded.

"I live on the third floor. The second room on the right. There will be many men who will offer to buy you a meal, but such meals never come for free. When you are so hungry that you think you cannot refuse them, remember that there is always a warm meal for you in Fabien's room." Suddenly she smiled. "But always knock first."

"Thank you," said Dany.

"And remember—when you're a little older and looking for work, come see me first. I may be running my own business by then, and I can always find work for pretty girls."

Fabien turned and began walking down the boulevard, but Dany stayed where she was, staring at the artist in rapt fascination. Why would such a wealthy man not have servants to help him when he got too drunk? Or a carriage, so he didn't have to walk at all? She'd seen street artists by the Seine, artists who could paint four portraits an hour for the tourists, and he certainly didn't look or dress like any of them. Maybe Fabien was wrong and he wasn't an artist at all.

But whatever he was, she felt sorry for him, having to walk on those horribly stunted legs. She stayed where she was for another moment, then decided it was time to find a cellar or stable in which to spend the night.

She had just started to walk away when she heard footsteps echoing down the wet street. She looked back down rue Frochot and saw a small, wiry man dressed in trousers and a striped jersey, with a red silk scarf around his neck and a beret on his head, walking down the street perhaps fifty yards away.

He's going to kill the artist! she thought.

And then, before she quite knew what she was doing, she ran to the fallen artist's side and knelt down next to him before the man in the beret had seen either of them. When he came within earshot, she began crying softly.

"What's the matter, girl?" he said, approaching her.

"My father!" wept Dany. "He fell down and hit his head on the street!"

The man laughed. "That's not your father. It's just Toulouse-Lautrec, dead drunk again." He stared at the unconscious artist. "They say it's going to rain before morning. If you're not robbing him yourself, if you really do know him, you'd better get him home."

"Me?" she said, surprised. "I don't know where he lives."

"Twenty-one rue Caulaincourt." He looked amused. "I think half of my girls have posed for him there at one time or another. I saw you talking to one of them a few minutes ago. She calls herself Fabien this week."

"This week?"

"It's not wise to use the same name for any length of time in Montmartre."

"Please, sir, can you tell me how to get the painter to his apartment?"

He looked down at Dany. "Can you read?"

She shook her head. "Just numbers, not words and letters."

"All right. I will tell you how to get there. And I want you to remember that Jacques Nicot is your friend, because when you get a little older, you are going to need a friend like me. I will protect you from all the vermin prowling the streets of Montmartre and put you to work, and we will both get so rich we can go to the same clubs and restaurants as the artist here."

He gave her directions, then headed off after Fabien, whistling a tune that was popular in the local clubs.

Dany put her hand under the artist's head and tried to move him to a sitting position. "Please wake up!" she said. "I'm not strong enough to lift you."

Suddenly the man's eyes fluttered open. "An angel!" he said dreamily, looking into her face. "I've died, and I'm in the arms of an angel."

Then he collapsed again.

Dany went through his pockets. She found a wad of francs, appropriated a few, and tucked them inside her left shoe. Then she grabbed his shoulders and shook him.

"Wake up!" she said. "Wake up or I'll leave you here!"

And almost upon command the man opened his eyes again. "Where am I?" he mumbled.

"In Montmartre."

"Of course I'm in Montmartre—but *where* in Montmartre?"

"In Pigalle," said Dany. "You tripped and fell."

"I did?"

"Yes. Can you get up?"

"Give me your hand, girl," said the man. She stretched out her hand to him. "Now pull."

It took three tries, but at last she got him to his feet.

"My cane," he said. "I need my cane."

She walked over and picked it up. He started swaying again, and she gave the cane to him just before he fell over once more.

"I realize this is going to sound strange," he said, "but I can't remember where I live."

"I can tell you where," she said. "But it's almost a mile. Can you walk that far?"

"I must have walked from there to here," he said, his speech slurred. "So of course I can walk back."

"But you weren't this drunk when you walked here," Dany pointed out.

"True," he agreed. "But I've just had a very refreshing nap on the street, and my strength has been renewed." He leaned toward her, trying to focus his eyes, and she had to catch him before he fell again.

"I'd better help you," said Dany.

"I would consider that a rare pleasure," he said. "As well as an absolute necessity." He reached above his head with his right hand and a puzzled frown crossed his face.

"Is something wrong?" she asked.

"I was going to take off my hat and bow to you," he answered.

"But I don't seem to have one. I could have sworn I had a hat when the evening began."

"You can worry about the hat tomorrow." She wanted to give his arm a tug to get him moving, but she was afraid that it might pull him over.

"You are right, of course," he said, nodding gravely. "Let us commence."

He stood still, looking down the boulevard de Clichy.

"What's the matter?" asked Dany.

"I'm not sure," he said, a puzzled frown on his face. "I think my feet are asleep."

"Both of them?"

"Poor circulation. Once I get moving, they'll work better. Here I go."

He leaned forward and seemed about to fall when he finally moved his left foot forward, then his right, and slowly, awkwardly, swaying not only from the alcohol but from the difficulty of walking on such misshapen legs, he started down the boulevard. Dany walked beside him, ready to support him if he lost his balance.

He had to stop every few minutes, not to catch his breath, but to wait for the pain in his legs to subside. At one point he turned to her and asked her name.

"Dany."

"A nice name," he said approvingly. "And you may call me Henri." He paused. "It must be nine o'clock already. Isn't it past your bedtime?"

"It will be dawn in two or three hours," she replied.

"Really?" he replied, surprised. "Where *has* the day gone?"

Dany didn't know how to answer him, so she remained silent, and soon they began walking again. It took another hour, and they were never free from prying eyes that studied them from the shadows, but finally they arrived at 21 rue Caulaincourt.

"Here is your apartment," Dany announced.

"My studio," he replied. "But I spend all my time here. I rarely go to my apartment anymore." Henri paused, staring at her. "You look as if you haven't eaten in a week. Come in, and we'll get you some food."

She stared at him suspiciously.

"What is the matter, child?" he said.

"I was warned about men who offer me meals."

"It's good advice," he said. "But I'm not going to feed you. The concierge is."

"Won't she be asleep?"

"She's used to my hours," he said without directly answering her. "Come along now."

She didn't move.

"Don't be afraid," he said. "You look disgustingly healthy. Even if I were sober, do you think I could catch any healthy woman who didn't want to be caught?"

She considered his statement for a long moment, and finally nodded her consent.

Henri reached into his pocket, then frowned. "We can't go in."

"Why not?"

"I don't have my key. I've been robbed."

"I was watching you. Nobody robbed you."

He scratched his head and pondered for a moment, then reached into his other pocket, muttered a satisfied "Ah" and withdrew a key. He made three shaky attempts to insert it into the lock and failed each time. Finally he gave it to Dany. She unlocked the door and followed him up the stairs, ready to break his fall if he tripped. At last they reached the studio.

"It is not a typical artist's garret," he said, trying without success to sound apologetic rather than amused. "I hope that does not disappoint you too greatly."

He opened the door.

"It's *huge!*" she said. "You must be *very* rich!"

"Wait right here," replied Henri. "I wouldn't want you bumping into anything." He shuffled around the room, lighting the lamps, and then signaled for her to enter.

She walked into the room, and suddenly she froze, her eyes wide, her mouth agape. Here was a painting of the elegant interior of a nightclub, there a palatial dance hall, over there a charming little café.

"Are these places real, or did you make them up?" she asked, staring at them in wonder.

"They're real."

"And they look like this?"

"More or less."

"It's like seeing another world!" she said.

"It *is* another world," said Henri. "My world." He stared at her, then smiled. "I suppose the very least I can do for the angel of mercy who saved me from waking up in the gutter is show that world to her. Would you like that?"

She nodded, unable to speak.

"Good," he said. "There is a bed in the next room. You will sleep in it." She started to protest, but he held up a hand. "You will be perfectly safe. I will sleep here on the couch by the window, and tomorrow Henri Toulouse-Lautrec will show his guardian angel the nightlife of Montmartre."

"Really?"

"Really. Now let us arrange for your food." He pounded on the floor with his cane, then smiled at her. "I'm just alerting the concierge. She'll be up with a hot meal for you and coffee for me."

"How will she know that I want a meal?"

"She will make both for me," he explained. "But I cannot face food tonight, so it is my gift to you."

"She will see me and demand that I leave," said Dany.

"Not if she wants her rent," said Henri with another smile.

"Believe me, you are not the first female to spend the night here. Although," he added thoughtfully, "you may be the first to sleep alone in the bedroom."

Dany began walking slowly around the room, not daring to touch the gilded chairs or plush sofa, and giving the delicate vase that sat on a marble stand a wide berth. She continued studying scenes of a world she had only vaguely imagined existed.

"And these women, the ones without enough clothes on—they are paid to dance?"

"Very handsomely."

Dany continued to stare at the paintings.

"Close your mouth, girl," said Henri, half flattered and half amused. "You never know what might fly into it."

But she was as oblivious of him as he had been of her while lying on the street in Pigalle.

CHAPTER TWO

A Restaurant in Montmartre

"I shouldn't try to go to any of those fancy places dressed like this," protested Dany the next afternoon when Henri had finally awakened from his drunken slumber. "They won't let me in."

"You will be with me, and that will get you into every restaurant and nightclub in Montmartre unchallenged," he answered. "I am not without some influence in such places."

"You spend that much money there?" she asked with wide eyed wonder.

"Well, that too," he admitted, "but I am the one who paints their posters."

"All of them?"

"No," he replied, "Just the good ones."

"You do not smile when you make a joke."

"That was not a joke. There are many things I cannot do, but I am very good at the few things I *can* do."

"Are your paintings in the Louvre?"

"Not yet."

"Maybe that's because so many of the women you paint have no clothes on," suggested Dany, gesturing to some of the paintings in question.

"Have you ever been to the Louvre?" asked Henri.

"No," she admitted, "but I have walked past it."

"Someday you must enter it; and when you do, I want you to count how many paintings there are of women with their clothes off."

"Your models must be very chilly when you are painting them," she observed, looking at a series of nudes.

"The thought of what I will pay them when I am finished keeps them warm."

"Maybe the sunlight helps warm them too," she said. "I have never been in such a bright room."

"I am an artist. I must have light."

She pointed to a trio of woodblock prints that seemed very different from all the others. "Did you paint these too?"

He shook his head. "No, I bought them. They are from Japan."

"Why does an artist buy another artist's paintings?"

"To learn from them," answered Henri. "They were totally different from anything anyone was doing here. The lines, the colors—they were unique before I began modifying the style of my own work."

Dany looked around the room once more. "Why do you not paint men with their clothes off?" she asked. "I don't see a single one."

He smiled. "I leave that to the female artists."

"Will the dancers have their clothes off tonight?"

"Eventually," answered Henri. "I imagine that it is very difficult to sleep in those outfits. But they will not take them off while they are performing."

"Good," said Dany. "I want to see the pretty clothes and the bright colors."

"And so you shall, guardian angel. But first we must eat dinner."

"Will the concierge cook it?"

"No, we will go to a restaurant."

A look of panic crossed her face. "I have never been to a restaurant before. I won't know what to do!"

"You will just sit opposite me, read the menu, and tell me what you would like to eat."

She lowered her gaze to the floor. "I can't read." It was strange: it didn't bother her to admit that to Jacques Nicot, but it was humiliating to confess it to this obviously educated man.

"No matter," he said, shrugging it off. "I'll order for both of us. Just tell me what kind of food you like."

"Nobody ever offered me a choice," answered Dany. "I just eat whatever is on the plate."

"Very reasonable," he said. "But tonight you will be able to choose exactly what you want."

"And this will be a *real* restaurant, like the ones I pass on the street?"

"Absolutely."

"You must be very rich," said Dany once again.

"I am."

"Then why aren't your paintings in the Louvre?"

"The one has nothing to do with the other," he replied. "I sell my paintings, and I have become much in demand as an artist. But it is not the paintings that make me rich, it is my name."

"It is a funny name," she said.

"Oh? Why?"

"Because Toulouse is a city, not a person."

"It is both," replied Henri. "I am a direct descendant of the counts of Toulouse. In fact, my mother is a countess."

"Are your parents still alive?"

"Yes. They live in Toulouse. I have not seen them since I moved here."

"Does all your family have such short little legs?"

He glared angrily at her for a moment, then realized that the question was asked out of childish curiosity.

"No," he said, "I broke my thighs when I was younger than you. They never healed properly."

"Are they still broken?" she asked, wide-eyed.

He shook his head. "No, but once my thighs were broken, my legs stopped growing."

"Do they hurt much?"

"From time to time."

"I am sorry," said Dany.

"So am I," Henri replied wryly. "Once I could run like the wind. Now I struggle not to let that same wind blow me over."

"*I* can run like the wind," volunteered Dany.

"I'm sure you can."

"But I think I'd rather be rich and a great painter. Or maybe just rich."

"Perhaps someday you shall be," said Henri.

"The dancers in your paintings—are *they* rich?"

"Most of them aren't."

"But a few are?" Dany persisted.

"A few," he conceded. "Not because they are better dancers than the others, but because my paintings have made them famous."

"Then someday perhaps you will paint me and make me famous."

"Anything's possible. But in the meantime, I think we are ready to go out for dinner."

"Before we do, I have a confession to make," said Dany.

"Oh?"

"I stole some francs from you when you were sleeping on the street last night. They are in my shoe. I have begged since my father left, but I have never stolen before. Please don't beat me."

She began to take off her shoe to get the money and return it, but Henri reached for her hand and pulled it away.

"I won't beat you," he said. "The francs are yours."

"But I stole them."

"And I stole your evening and morning," said Henri. "Now we are even."

"Then how will I repay you for dinner?"

"You are a very strange little beggar girl," he noted. "Those who live by their wits in Montmartre do not usually possess anything as bothersome as consciences. Since you obviously have one, it is clear that despite your current unhappy circumstance you did not grow up on the streets—or among the nobility, for that matter." He placed a hand on her shoulder. "My life is worth more than a hundred dinners, and it might well have been taken away from me last night had you not come to my aid. My house and my food are yours for as long as you care to avail yourself of them. I ask nothing in return, except that should I once again be in the condition that you observed last night—and I blush to admit that it happens quite often—you help me back to the studio before I can be robbed or killed. Do we have an agreement?"

She extended her hand. "Yes."

He shook her hand gravely, then leaned over and examined it closely. "When was the last time you washed?"

She shrugged. "I don't know."

"It is unhealthy not to bathe. Dinner can wait. First you will climb into the tub and clean yourself."

"You will not watch me or paint me while I am bathing?" she asked apprehensively.

He laughed. "Perhaps I will paint you someday, but only with your clothes on. That is my promise to you."

She went off to bathe, and he picked up a brush and began touching up the mouth and nose on one of the dancers whom he had painted the previous afternoon. He worked with short, fast, sure strokes and had completed her shoes by the time Dany emerged.

"Much better," he said as she presented her hands and face for inspection. "Tomorrow we will go shopping and buy you some better clothes, but it is too late today. All the shops are closed."

"Who is that?" asked Dany, pointing to the image of the blonde woman on which he was working.

"La Goulue."

"The Glutton?" she said, laughing. "That is really her name?"

"That is the name she uses when she dances," replied Henri. "I don't recall if she created it or the audience did, but it fits her. You will see her later tonight."

"She is very pretty," said Dany, "but she does not look exactly like this."

"How do you know?" he asked. "You have never seen her."

"That is true. But there is something different about your paintings." She paused. "I think maybe it is the colors; people and places are not so bright. Or perhaps it is that La Goulue is moving, and in all the other pictures I have ever seen, the people are always sitting or standing still."

"These are paintings, not photographs. I paint them the way they look in here," he said, tapping his temple with a forefinger. "Or perhaps," he continued thoughtfully, "I paint them the way they *should* look. If you are really interested, we can discuss it tomorrow. But we'd better go now, or they will sell my table out from under me."

"You *own* a table in a restaurant?" she asked, impressed.

"The restaurant owns the table, but they hold it for me every night until seven o'clock. If I do not arrive by then, they allow someone else to sit there."

"Then what do you do?"

He smiled. "I go to another restaurant where they hold my table until eight."

"It must be wonderful to be rich."

"It has its advantages," he agreed. "But I would trade it to be able to run like the wind like a young girl I know. Or even to walk without pain, for that matter." He stood up carefully. "Shall we go?"

He opened the door for her and slowly, laboriously followed her down the stairs and out into the street. She was about fifteen yards

ahead of him when she remembered that he could not walk at a normal speed, and she stopped until he caught up with her, then matched
her pace to his. She was aware that they made a very strange-looking
couple, an ill-clad girl and an elegantly dressed bearded gentleman
with a severe deformity. People stopped to look, but no one said anything—at least nothing that she could hear—and finally they reached
the restaurant.

A *maître d'* tried very hard not to stare at her as he ushered them
to Henri's table and handed them each a menu. Dany felt over-
whelmed by the luxury of her surroundings. The walls were covered
with flocked paper, the chairs had brocade cushions and gilt legs, the
entire dining room was carpeted, and the knives, forks, and spoons
positively gleamed as they caught the light.

"What am I to do with this?" she asked, indicating the menu.

"Pretend to read it."

"But I don't know how," she said. "I told you that already."

"It will be our secret."

She did as he suggested until he made his decision and put his
menu down on the table, and she followed suit. A waiter immediately appeared.

"Cognac for me, and the house white wine for the young lady,"
said Henri with an air of authority. "We will begin with caviar, next a
salad, and then the duckling with wild rice."

The waiter scurried off.

"Where is he going?" asked Dany.

"To tell the chef what we want. Then he will return with our
drinks."

"Oh." She looked around the room nervously.

"What's the matter, Dany?"

"People are staring at me," she said. "I shouldn't be wearing these clothes in a palace like this."

"They are staring because they know my taste in female companions, and you do not fit it." He shrugged. "Pay no attention to them."

The waiter returned with two glasses, one of cognac, one of wine.

"You forgot the bottle," said Henri.

"I beg your pardon, M. Lautrec?" said the waiter.

"The bottle of cognac."

"But you yourself told me never to—"

"I paid for the damage, didn't I?" said Henri harshly. "Now get the bottle!"

The waiter bowed and went off again.

"What happened the last time he brought you an entire bottle?" asked Dany.

"Nothing that couldn't be cleaned up," said Henri with a shrug. "Drink your wine and don't worry about it."

She sipped the wine. She had been drinking wine most of her life, but not like this. It tasted like some magic elixir, light and airy. She'd had no idea wine could go down so smoothly.

A moment later a well-dressed diner got up to leave and paused briefly as he passed their table. "You like them younger and younger, Henri," he said with a wink.

The artist raised his hand above his head and snapped his fingers. "Pierre-Paul!" he said in a loud voice.

The *maître d'* rushed over.

"Yes, M. Lautrec?" he asked solicitously.

"That man who just left here," began Henri.

"M. Duval?"

"That's the one. He just insulted this young lady."

"Say no more, M. Lautrec," said Pierre-Paul the *maître d'*. "He shall not be allowed back. Please accept my deepest apology."

Henri nodded and waved him away. "There must be a consequence for bad manners," he said to Dany. "Always remember that."

"I thought he insulted *you*, not *me*," she replied.

"He flattered me. The insult was to you, for he implied that a girl such as you would find a cripple like me . . ." He shrugged. "Let it pass."

"I do not understand."

"Someday soon you will, more's the pity," said Henri, closing the subject.

The waiter returned, bowed obsequiously, and placed the bottle in front of Henri.

"Don't drink it all," said Dany. "At least not right now. You promised to take me to a nightclub, and I don't want you to pass out before we get there."

He stared at her with a curious smile. "You *look* like my guardian angel," he said, "but you *sound* like my mother."

"Please."

He sighed. "All right. Two glasses now and one after dinner. Then nothing until I have fulfilled my promise to you."

"Good! Where are we going?" she asked eagerly.

"To the finest club in all Montmartre."

"What is it called?"

"The Moulin Rouge."

"The Red Mill? I never heard of it until last week."

An expression that was halfway between confidence and arrogance appeared on Henri's face.

"Before I'm through, all of Paris will hear of it."

CHAPTER THREE

A Nightclub in Montmartre

They walked down the boulevard de Clichy, with Henri nodding to an occasional well-dressed acquaintance and pointing out clubs and restaurants to Dany.

"This is not like Pigalle at all," remarked Dany. "Everybody is well dressed, and the thieves and prostitutes are nowhere to be seen."

"They're around nonetheless," answered Henri. "But like bats and werewolves, they tend not to come out before midnight." He looked ahead. "We will be there in another block. You can see the windmill from here."

"I have walked past it," answered the girl, "but I never dreamed that I would enter it."

"We won't go inside right away," he said with a smile.

"But you promised!"

"Oh, we'll enter, but I think you will want to see the yard first."

"A yard is a yard," she said. "I grew up on a farm. What can there be in a city yard that I haven't seen?"

"I don't believe I'm going to tell you," said Henri.

"There are so many people going in. Are you sure there will be room for us?"

"I have my own table."

"Just like at the restaurant?"

"Exactly," replied Henri. "I am a creature of habit."

"One of those habits is going to kill you," said Dany.

"I thought you were a guardian angel, not a guardian watchdog," he said wryly.

"Why are we stopping?" she asked as he came to a halt while still a half block from the club.

"I need to rest," he replied. "I'll be all right in a minute."

"Have you seen a doctor?"

"Over the years I have kept a half dozen of them in caviar," he said. "There is nothing to be done for me. I suppose I should be thankful that I can walk at all." He took a deep breath and released it slowly. "All right, we can proceed."

Music came out to them from most of the clubs.

"It sounds like everyone is having a good time," she said. "Do all the clubs have dancers?"

He shook his head. "A few do. Most just have music, and the patrons themselves do the dancing."

"But the Moulin Rouge has the dancers you painted?"

"Most of them dance there, yes."

"Good."

"Why 'good'?"

"Because no one I've seen is wearing the colorful dresses you painted, and I want to see them."

"You shall," he said, stepping around a drunken man who was getting rid of his dinner at the edge of the sidewalk.

A hard-looking woman passed by them. "There but for the grace of God go you, Henri," she said with a smile, pointing at the man.

"Nonsense," answered the artist, "it's much too early in the evening for me to be in that condition."

She laughed and continued walking.

"Do you know her?" asked Dany.

"I suppose so."

"You *suppose* so?"

"It's difficult to remember all the women I meet after dark in Montmartre," he said. "Ah, here we are."

The flashing lights seemed even brighter, and the girl suddenly noticed a faux Gothic castle right next to the club.

"It looks like monsters live there," she said, indicating the castle.

"Probably they do," said Henri, amused. "Monsters live all over Montmartre."

"Are you sure we can't go right in?" asked Dany eagerly, staring in awe at the elegantly-clad patrons entering the building.

"Soon," he said,"but let us go around the back first."

She saw a small group of people walking around the building to a fenced yard and fell into step behind them. Suddenly she could hear a strange chattering she had never encountered before, punctuated by an occasional shriek.

"What was that?" she asked.

"Monkeys," answered Henri. "Haven't you ever seen one before?"

"No."

"Well, there are dozens of them roaming around the yard."

"Really?" said Dany excitedly. "I want to see them! Is there anything else back there?"

Henri merely smiled and made no answer.

It was all Dany could do not to leave him and race ahead, but she applied considerable self-restraint and walked to the enclosed yard beside him, then turned to her left.

"Oh, *mon Dieu*!" she exclaimed. "Is it alive?"

"No," answered Henri.

"It is an elephant, isn't it?" asked Dany. "My mother told me about them."

"It is a wooden model of one, with papier-mâché skin. Although no elephant has ever been quite this large."

The elephant stood almost twenty feet at the shoulder. Off to its left side was a stage, and a chorus of six women were singing and dancing on it while some forty men and women sat on rows of lawn chairs, watching the show.

"What is *that*?" asked Dany, pointing to an open portal in one of the elephant's legs, where an elderly man in a top hat was just entering.

"It's a spiral staircase leading to a room in the elephant's stomach."

"Now, why would he want to go into the elephant's stomach?" said Dany.

"There is a much smaller show going on there," answered Henri. "There are belly dancers imported all the way from Turkey. And, for a price, opium." He paused thoughtfully. "I believe the opium costs more than the show, but I could be mistaken."

"What is a belly dancer?" she asked. "Can we see them?"

He shook his head. "Women are not allowed to enter the elephant's stomach," said Henri. "Unless, of course, they are belly dancers."

"That doesn't seem very fair," complained Dany.

"Your family is dead, you beg on the streets of Montmartre to stay alive, and you are surprised that life isn't fair?"

A monkey scampered up to them and began chattering.

"What does he want?" asked Dany.

"He is another member of the begging fraternity," explained the artist. He pulled a grape out of his pocket. "Here," he said, handing it to her. "I knew we would be coming here, so I brought this along. Give it to him."

"Will he bite?"

"Only if you don't feed him," said Henri with a chuckle. "He has much in common with human beggars."

She took the grape, crouched down, and held it out. The monkey took it and raced off, and suddenly she was surrounded by monkeys.

"Have you any more grapes?" she asked over the din of their chattering.

"No," said Henri, as the monkeys pressed forward aggressively. "They are like the beggars of Montmartre. Once you give one of them something, there's no end to it." He summoned an attendant and paid him a franc to drive away the monkeys. "Shall we go into the club now?"

"In just a minute," she said, staring at the elephant and the stage show.

"I thought you were anxious to go inside."

"I am," said Dany. "But I may never come back to the Moulin

Rouge, and I want to make sure I remember what this part of it looks like. I didn't see it in any of your paintings."

"I paint people," replied Henri. "I leave elephants and monkeys to others."

"Did you paint the belly dancers?"

He shook his head. "I cannot climb the stairs."

She looked around for another few seconds, then turned to him. "All right," she said.

They walked back to the front of the building. There was a small line of people still waiting to enter; but a tall, lean man walked out of the club, greeted Henri like a long-lost brother, and led him and Dany inside the Moulin Rouge, down a plush red hallway.

"Dany, this is Joseph Oller, the man who built the Moulin Rouge," said Henri. "Joseph, this guardian angel is the reason I'm alive and well today."

"She momentarily rescued you from your worst tendencies, of course," said Oller. He turned to Dany. "I am very pleased to meet you, Mademoiselle Angel," he said, bowing low and kissing her hand. "I would hate to lose my friend Henri—especially when he still owes me the most expensive poster I have ever commissioned."

"All in good time," said the artist. "I am still studying the premises."

"If you were a Medusa, the premises would have turned to stone long ago," said Oller with a laugh.

"I love your monkeys!" blurted Dany.

"I wish everyone felt that way, young Angel," said Oller. "They are so much easier to deal with than my dancers." He smiled at Henri. "Sometimes I think I should have been a zookeeper instead."

"Sometimes I think you are," replied Henri, and Oller almost doubled over with laughter. "I will be happy to trade observations with you all night, Joseph," he continued after a moment, "but I find standing uncomfortable. Why don't you join us at our table?"

"I apologize, my friend," said Oller, leading them to an empty table right next to the large dance floor. "I have things to attend to. I will join you later."

He pulled out a chair for Dany, who merely stared at him curiously.

"Sit, Dany," said Henri after a moment.

She sat down, confused. "I thought it was for you, M. Oller."

"Has no one ever held out a chair for you?" asked Oller.

"Only tonight. But he was a waiter, so I knew he wasn't going to sit with us."

"When you get a little older, men will fight to hold chairs and open doors for you, Angel," said Oller. He turned to Henri. "I'll be by later."

He wandered off, and Dany finally had a chance to look around. There was a huge wooden dance floor in the middle of the room, quite large enough to accommodate four hundred couples. Totally surrounding it were one hundred and fifty tables covered with white linen, overlooking the dance floor and rising in tiers. Clearly there was a kitchen somewhere, because there was food on a number of the tables, though the majority held only drinks. There was a polished bar the length of the room along one wall, and opposite it was a roped-off area holding a band that included brass, woodwinds, strings, drums, and a piano. All the musicians, like the waiters, were clad in formal dress.

Finally there were four wide, diagonal aisles leading from the corners of the room to the dance floor. They seemed to be much wider than the waiters required, and Dany asked Henri about them.

"You'll see," he said. "And now, what would you like to drink?"

"I don't know," she said. "White wine, I suppose, like I had at dinner."

"This time it will be white wine filled with bubbles," said Henri. "In other words, champagne. You may have only one glass, because I suspect I will be in no condition to help you walk home—but everyone should have champagne the first time they come to the Moulin Rouge."

"I have never had champagne before."

"Then the experience will be all the more memorable." He held his hand in the air and snapped his fingers, and a waiter instantly appeared.

"Good evening, M. Lautrec," he said. "I'm glad to see you are feeling well today. We had some concern for you when you left last night."

"Your concern is heartwarming," said Henri sardonically. "I will have my usual, and the young lady will have a glass of your best champagne."

"We go through this every night, M. Lautrec," said the waiter. "Which is your usual—cognac or absinthe?"

"I'll be damned if I know," replied Henri. "Bring a bottle of each."

"Are you quite sure, M. Lautrec?" asked the waiter in a concerned tone.

"It's all right," said Henri. "What I don't drink I'll take home and feed to the cat."

"You don't own a cat."

"Then I'll find one," replied the artist.

The waiter sighed, nodded his head, and walked off.

"The women are so beautifully dressed!" said Dany, looking at the audience. "I almost don't care if we see the dancers or not. I could spend all night looking at the ladies who are seated at the tables!"

The band began warming up, and Henri smiled at her. "Tell me that in fifteen minutes."

"I like that music," said Dany, tapping her fingers on the table.

"It is by a man named Offenbach," said Henri, pulling out a sketchbook.

"He doesn't sound French."

"He wasn't," answered Henri. "But his *music* is."

He began drawing a sketch of Dany; but before he could get much of it done, there was a shrill scream from the farthest corner of the room, followed by matching yells from the other three corners. A few seconds later can-can dancers began racing down the four broad, diagonal aisles to the dance floor. Dressed in brilliant colors—reds and yellows and blues—they joined arms and began their dance, then spread out and performed a series of cartwheels.

"Look at that one!" said an awestruck Dany. "She is walking across the floor on her hands!"

"That's Nini-le-Belle-en-Cuisse," said Henri.

"Nini of the Beautiful Thighs?" replied Dany. "That is a very rude name."

The artist smiled. "Her skirt is over her head. They call her Nina-le-Belle-en-Cuisse because her thighs are about the only part of her you can see when she's performing. She is actually quite proud of the name."

"You have painted her?"

"Of course."

"The beautiful one," said Dany, pointing to a slender, dark-haired woman who seemed to stand out from the others. "Who is she?"

"Jane Avril."

"Have you painted her too?"

"A few times. But I am not pleased with the results. Someday I will do her justice."

The waiter delivered Dany's glass of champagne and Henri's bottles and glasses.

"Just take small sips," Henri instructed her.

He poured himself a glass of cognac; but before he could drink it, a hefty dancer stopped by the table, raised her leg until it rested on his shoulder, took the glass away from him, and downed its contents.

"*Bonsoir, mon cheri!*" she said. "You have a new partner tonight."

"*Bonsoir,*" he replied. Suddenly he grinned. "Unlike you, this one I can afford to feed."

She threw back her head and laughed. "I will be back when you open the absinthe," she promised, dancing over to another table and taking a bite of the pastry there.

"Let me guess," said Dany. "That is La Goulue."

"As gluttonous as ever," answered Henri.

"She is not very pretty," said Dany. "And Jane Avril and some of the others are more graceful. Why is she so famous?"

"Because of me."

"Will *I* become famous if you paint me?"

"Anything's possible."

She fell silent, watching the dancers in rapt fascination as they whirled around the floor, filling the air with their exuberant cries. Before long they formed a line and began their high-kicking, then one by one they threw themselves in the air and landed on the floor doing splits. Finally the dance was over, and the girls ran up the aisles (though La Goulue managed to grab two more drinks along the way).

Joseph Oller walked over and pulled up a chair as the band played a slower song and most of the patrons left their tables to dance.

"So, Henri," he said, "have you decided upon the poster yet?"

"I'm working on it," replied the artist noncommittally.

Oller turned to Dany. "And you, Mademoiselle Angel, did you enjoy the show?"

"Oh, yes!" enthused Dany. "It was the most beautiful and exciting thing I've ever seen!"

"I am delighted that you have enjoyed your visit to the Moulin Rouge."

"When I am older I am going to dance in your show!" she said.

"At the rate Louise is eating, there may be an opening very soon," said Oller.

"Louise?" she said, puzzled.

"La Goulue," he explained. "Her real name is Louise Weber."

"Do you really want to work here?" Henri asked her.

"More than anything!" said Dany.

The artist turned to Oller. "Tragedy has befallen this young lady's family, and she finds herself in dire economic straits. Do you think you can find work for her at the club?"

"She is a little young for a dancer," said Oller, studying her.

"What about waiting on tables?"

"All of our waiters are men," said Oller. He stared at Dany, study-ing her. "But perhaps we can find some work for her cleaning the tables, and of course the dancers are always clamoring for more maids and dressers."

"I will work for free!" said Dany excitedly.

"You are already working for free," said Henri. "It is time to improve your position."

Oller continued staring at her. "All right," he said, "we'll find something for her to do. Two francs a week, and she can have her meals in the kitchen."

"Four francs," said Henri promptly.

Oller turned and studied the artist as carefully as he had studied the girl. "I will make you a deal," he said at last. "It will be four francs a week—but you and I will split her salary fifty-fifty until you deliver my poster. Once it is done, I will pay her entire salary." He grinned happily. "*That* should encourage you to stop thinking and start painting."

Henri extended his hand and shook on it. "I agree to your terms."

"Report here at four o'clock tomorrow, Mademoiselle Angel," said Oller, getting to his feet and walking across the dance floor to another table.

"Did he mean it?" asked Dany.

"He meant it."

"I'm really going to work here!" she said, unable to sit still. "Thank you so much, Henri!"

"Finish your champagne now," he said, putting his sketchbook back into a pocket. "It's time to go."

"But the dancers will perform again in a few minutes, won't they?"

"You are an employee of the Moulin Rouge now. You can see them every night."

"Are we going to another club then?"

He shook his head. "No," he replied. "We are going back to the studio."

"The studio?" she said, unable to hide her disappointment. "Why?"

He sighed deeply. "It seems that I have a poster to create."

A Lesson in Montmartre

"Isn't it too late to start painting?" asked Dany as they entered the studio. "I thought you needed the sunlight to see the colors properly."

"I do."

"Well, then?"

"I will not be painting tonight," explained Henri. "First I must decide what the poster will look like, who will be in it, how they will be posed—though I hate the word pose, because it sounds so stiff and formal. I must work out all the details; and then I will sketch what I am doing, first in pencil, then in ink; and finally I will prepare the finished product for the lithographer." He paused thoughtfully. "In fact, I will not be painting at all."

"I don't understand," said Dany. "Weren't you supposed to paint a poster for M. Oller?"

"That is *his* word," answered Henri. "But if I were to create a painting, he would not be happy with me, because then it would hang, unique and solitary, inside the club. He has commissioned me to create a poster, which means there will be hundreds, probably thousands, on walls and signboards all over Paris." He smiled at her. "Did you think I was going to paint the same thing a thousand times?"

"I don't know," she admitted. "I never thought about it."

"There is no reason why you should," he replied. "After all, you are an employee of the Moulin Rouge. It is I who must make it so famous that they can pay your extravagant salary."

"When I am a famous can-can dancer like La Goulue and Jane Avril, I will make lots of money," she said. "Maybe someday I will even buy the Moulin Rouge myself."

"You are not going to be a can-can dancer," said Henri firmly. "This job is temporary, until I can find you a better position in polite society."

"But I like it there!" she protested. "It's lively and colorful, and everyone seems so happy! And the dancers live such exciting lives!"

"You think so, do you?"

"I know what I saw," said Dany stubbornly.

"Those can-can dancers you so admire," said Henri, "almost every one of them was a prostitute by the time she was fifteen. Half of them are drug addicts. More than half will die before they're thirty years old. It is no life for a sweet girl from a farm."

"But—"

"We'll speak no more of it," said the artist. "That is your future if you become a dancer in Montmartre, and I will not have it on my conscience." He laid a gentle hand on her shoulder. "I know it seems cruel to you right now, but the day will come when you thank me."

He shuffled over to a closet, withdrew a large rectangular sheet of paper that was somewhere between cream and pale tan, and affixed it to his easel. Then he rummaged through a box of pens, charcoals, and pencils until he found a thick pencil with very soft lead.

"You're going to make a poster just with that?" asked Dany.

"I'm not going to make a poster until I'm through with that," he replied. "Before the colors and the figures and the letters comes the composition, the choice of what I will put in the poster and exactly where I will put it." He turned to her. "Perhaps you can help."

"How?"

"Once I decide what I am surrounding her with, you can be La Goulue—though you're about three inches too short and sixty pounds too light."

"Then La Goulue is to be in the center of the poster?" asked Dany.

"She is the biggest star in the show," answered Henri. "It would be foolhardy to draw someone the public *doesn't* come to see."

"You have four paintings of her in the studio already," Dany pointed out. "Two with her clothes off, two with them on. Why do you need me to pretend to be La Goulue when you have them already?"

"Those were portraits," he explained. "She is either sitting still or standing still or lying down. But this is a poster. It has to give the feeling of the cancan, so I need to capture her in motion." He paused. "Have you looked at those Japanese prints I purchased?"

"Yes."

"They had the right idea, those Japanese artists—bold lines, bold colors, and always a feeling of motion." His face reflected his admiration. "The robes flow, the hair floats in the wind, the feet are never planted squarely beneath the body. I have improved upon the artists technique, but it is simply an extension of the direction they pointed to."

"So you will paint me kicking my foot above my head?" asked Dany uncertainly. "I don't know if I can do it. I certainly cannot hold such a pose long enough for you to capture it with your pencil."

"I don't *want* you to hold a pose," replied Henri. "When the time comes, I will tell you how to move; and I will decide which instant in time I will put on the poster. But of course the poster must have many other things, or rather the *hint* of many other things. The Moulin Rouge is famous for its dancers, but it is much more than that."

"How do you give hints in a single poster?" she asked curiously.

"Oh, there are many ways," he said. "I could show a line of dancers in the background, so people will know how large and impressive the show is. I could show a crowd of admiring men, all in their tophats. Or I could put a few women in the crowd to show that they are welcome too. I could put the band in one corner and the polished bar in another. I could have a waiter bringing out a whole lobster, so people will know that they can order food as well as drink." Suddenly he grinned. "I might even put Joseph Oller in the picture, so that he will be reluctant to tell me to change it. Or," he added, "I might put in the real genius behind the show."

"I thought that was M. Oller," said Dany.

Henri shook his head. "No, he is the man who built it, and he is the owner, but he has a partner, Charles Zidler, who selects and trains the girls. I suppose one would call him the choreographer, though he is much more. He selects the costumes, chooses all the colors, even selects the Offenbach pieces they dance to. That's why you didn't meet him tonight. He is always backstage, watching the dancers, ready to make any changes or corrections that are needed before the next show."

"It sounds like a wonderful job."

"It is. They say he's the one who changed the dance's name to can-can. When I first came to town, it was known as the *quadrille realiste*."

"I like can-can much better."

"So does everyone else," agreed Henri. He turned back to his easel. "Now, if this were a painting, I would configure it differently; but it is a poster, which is very much like a book cover. I must leave room at the top for the title, or in this case the name of the club, and a little more room for the address. I won't put in the prices, because if this poster does what I hope it will do, Joseph will be raising his prices very soon, and we wouldn't want any outraged patrons pointing to the prices on the poster." He stared at the blank paper and made a sweeping arc about three-quarters of the way up.

"What is that?"

"Nothing yet," he replied. "But eventually it will be a row of dancers or a row of patrons."

"But it goes off the paper on both sides," she said. "Whoever you're drawing, shouldn't you have them clustered together so people can see them all?"

"Why?"

She shrugged. "I don't know. That's the way all the paintings I have ever seen have looked."

"Stand six feet from the window," said Henri.

She walked over to where he indicated.

"Now look straight out."

"All right," she said. "I am looking straight out."

"What do you see?"

"The lights of Montmartre, and a tree in the next yard."

"Very good," said Henri. "Now, what *don't* you see?"

Dany frowned. "I don't understand."

"You're looking straight ahead," he said. "You see the yard and some lights. But you don't see the walls on each side of you. You're too close to the window to see where that wall joins the others."

"All right, I don't see the walls. So what?"

"But you know they're there, do you not?" he persisted. "You know that the wall that holds the window extends for many feet in each direction and that it joins two other walls of the studio. If you stepped back ten or twelve feet, you could probably see those corners."

"I know that."

"Now, if you were painting what you see, would you change the shape of the room so that you could paint the corners, and show the walls on each side of you?"

"No."

"Very good, Dany," he said. "Your eye is like a camera. It sees what you are looking at, and if what you are looking at is too big, it sees only part of it. I paint the way my eye sees. If there is a man standing at the corner of my vision, I paint the part of him I can see and do not pretend to guess what the rest of him looks like. If I am standing close to him and staring at his face, his legs are below my field of vision and I do not paint them."

"But nobody paints like that."

"*I* paint like that," replied Henri. "And soon others will too. You are too young to realize it, but there is a revolution going on right now."

"I haven't heard any gunfire," said Dany.

"This revolution is being fought with brushes rather than with bullets, but it is a revolution nonetheless. I had a friend, Vincent, who created paintings such as no one had ever seen. And the greatest artist currently working in Paris is Edgar Degas, who does not even use paint but colored chalks! I paint scenes and people that all other artists disdain. Yes, we are overthrowing the old order of the art world. Even this poster I am to create will not be the work of a commercial hack but of a dedicated artist who needs no patron and is not ashamed to be well paid for his work." He realized that he had been almost shouting in his enthusiasm, and he paused for a moment, then continued in a more conversational tone of voice. "As I told you before: there are hundreds of things that are beyond my capabilities, but the things I can do I do very well indeed." A self-deprecating smile crossed his face. "So far they number two: painting and drinking."

"If you drank less, you would be sober longer and would be able to paint more."

"That is true," he admitted. "On the other hand, I have already completed more than three hundred paintings. Do you know how many the great Leonardo da Vinci completed in his life?"

"No."

"About a dozen. If I didn't drink I'd have completed four hundred instead of three hundred, and who would know the difference?"

"It is not good for your health."

"But perhaps it is good for my art," he countered. "When I am drunk, I see colors no one else has ever seen."

"When you are drunk, you are incapable of painting them," she responded.

"Touché," he said with a smile. "You have no fear of me at all, have you?"

"Why should I be afraid?" asked Dany. "You have treated me better than anyone else I've ever known."

"I shall try to live up to your high opinion of me. Now, back to work."

He stared at the semicircle he had drawn, then put a large oval in the very center of the picture.

"What is that?" asked Dany.

"Now it is an oval, which is merely a circle that's had too much to drink. Soon it will be my guardian angel, and eventually it will be La Goulue," answered Henri. "She is the centerpiece of the show and the poster, so she must be placed in the center. But of course I won't have her looking directly at the viewer. That would be too posed. I'll have her dancing for—" he studied the easel "—for the men who are stranding in the background."

"But then her back will be to the viewer!" said Dany.

"You saw her dance tonight. Was there ever a period as long as fifteen seconds when you were not able to see her front, her side, and her back?"

"No," said Dany, surprised. "No, there wasn't."

"Then she will not be ignoring our millions of viewers."

"Millions?" she repeated.

"Well, tens of thousands, anyway," he replied with a smile.

He studied the simple lines he had drawn, as if seeing a picture taking shape in his head. "Now, the dance floor is in the middle of the club. It is surrounded on all four sides, so as to show that there must be someone in the foreground." He drew a square just below the oval that represented La Goulue. "No, that won't do. Too static, too balanced." He crossed it out with a large X, then stared at it and frowned.

"What is the matter?" asked Dany.

"Nothing is the matter. I'm thinking."

"You look like your stomach hurts. Or maybe your head."

"They're thinking too."

She laughed. "How can a stomach think?"

"You'd be surprised at what a stomach can do," said Henri. "It can communicate, because it tells you when it is empty, or too full, or sick. It can speak to others, by rumbling and making embarrassing noises when you least want it to. It can even dance, as it proves every night inside the Moulin Rouge's elephant. No, never underestimate the stomach."

"How can a belly dance?"

He smiled bitterly. "You will have to get someone who is capable of climbing the stairs inside the elephant's leg to tell you." He reached out toward the easel, seemed about to draw something, then pulled back his hand. "You know what would be interesting?" he said, more to himself than to Dany. "What if I were to put a man in the foreground, much larger and closer than La Goulue but posed in such a way that he was looking at La Goulue, so that even if he was the first thing you saw, you would follow his gaze and your eyes would be drawn to her?" He stared off into space, visualizing what he had just described. "Wouldn't that be something if it worked?"

And suddenly he put a large rectangle at the right side of the drawing, beginning at the bottom and reaching almost as high as the top of the oval that represented La Goulue.

"She is not a tall woman," noted Dany. "Yet this man looks only a few inches taller, and he's standing beside her." She studied the paper thoughtfully. "Perhaps you need a bigger man. If he's wearing a tophat, he might even be smaller than she is."

"That's because they're an oval and a rectangle," explained Henri. "But when they become a man and a woman, things will be very different. Remember our example of the wall? He will be so close to the viewers that they will see him only from the waist up. That will show them how large the dance floor is, because they will see her dancing between him and the men in the back; and the perspective of each will give a fair representation of the size of the place." He continued studying his simplistic shapes. "It needs something else, something on the left, but I don't know what." He shrugged. "Ah, well, it will come to me tomorrow, I am sure."

He put the pencil back into the box.

"Aren't you going to draw me?" asked Dany, trying unsuccessfully to hide her eagerness.

"Soon," he said. "I need to fill out the structure first."

"Perhaps it is just as well," she said thoughtfully. "I can borrow one of the cancan costumes from the Moulin Rouge. I'm sure they'll loan it to me when I explain it is for the poster."

"That won't be necessary."

"But I'd *like* to wear a can-can dress."

"I am creating a poster of La Goulue," he said. "Any dress she has could cover two of you. Maybe three."

"Perhaps I could borrow one from Mademoiselle Avril, and you could say it was La Goulue's."

"No," he said firmly. "You are a sweet, pristine angel. I don't know why you are so fascinated by the tawdriest aspects of Montmartre."

"Aren't you?" she shot back.

He had no answer for that.

CHAPTER FIVE

A Star in Montmartre

Dany arrived at the Moulin Rouge promptly at four o'clock the next afternoon.

"You cannot come into the club," said the burly doorman, barring her way.

"But I work here!" she said.

He stared at her. "I have never seen you dance."

"I am not a dancer."

"If you are selling your favors, you are too young; and besides, it is too early in the day. We do not open to the public for another two hours."

"I am selling nothing!" she insisted heatedly. "I was hired by M. Oller."

"Sure you were. Now run along."

"What is the problem?" asked a feminine voice from behind her.

"Good afternoon, Mademoiselle Avril," said the doorman. "I was just sending this beggar on her way."

"I saw you last night," said Dany. "I was with Henri, the little crippled painter."

"M. Toulouse-Lautrec?" said Jane Avril, surprised.

"Yes. And M. Oller offered me a job. I was told to show up at four o'clock."

"You do not look like a dancer to me," said Jane Avril, studying the girl.

"I'm not. I was told I would clean tables and help the dancers get into their costumes."

"A *dresser*?" exclaimed Jane happily. "Why didn't you say so in the first place? Come with me!" She turned to the doorman. "It is all right, Pierre. Let her through."

"But—"

"I have told you to let her through. Do you really want me as your enemy?" she asked sweetly but with a hint of steel beneath it.

Pierre the doorman stood aside, and Jane and Dany passed through to the interior of the Moulin Rouge. "Come with me," said the dancer, hurrying to the dressing area. "If Oller sees you, he might take you away to sweep and mop the floors, or spread linens on the tables."

"Yes, Mademoiselle," said Dany, quickening her pace to keep up with Jane Avril.

They walked down a long, narrow passageway, finally emerging into a large dressing room that was filled with mirrors, makeup, and clothing racks.

"Safe!" breathed Jane happily. "The last time Oller came in here, La Goulue hit him and Nini kicked him." She turned to Dany. "What is your name, ma petite Mademoiselle?"

"Dany—and you are Jane Avril."

The dancer smiled. "Well, I am now."

Dany looked around the room. "How many dresses do you wear during the evening?"

"Usually just one, unless I sweat too much," answered Jane. "But I may ruin two or even three pairs of stockings. And I break a heel on a shoe on the average of twice a week."

"I do not know how to repair shoes or stockings," said Dany apologetically.

"No one expects you to. You are a dresser, not a cobbler or a seamstress."

"Do your dresses ever tear?"

"Hardly ever," answered Jane. "Only *la grosse vache* is eating herself out of her dresses."

"The fat cow?" asked Dany, though she thought she knew the answer.

"Louise Weber—though whoever named her La Goulue was more than perceptive. She is a glutton for everything—for food, for drink, for men." She smiled in amusement. "The woman is a walking appetite."

"Do you all wear the same dresses?"

"La Goulue could never fit into my dresses."

"I mean, the same patterns and colors?"

"Yes, the dancers do—although they change every month."

Dany pointed to a light green gown. "That one seems different. There are no others of that color."

"That belongs to Yvette Guilbert," answered Jane Avril. A look of condescension spread across her face. "She is merely a singer."

"I thought singers were important."

"Men do not pay to come to the Moulin Rouge to listen to chanteuses," said Jane with a smile. "They come to watch the dancers. Most particularly, they come to watch me."

"That is a matter of opinion," said a voice from the door.

Dany turned and saw the hefty figure of La Goulue approaching them.

"And who is this?" asked La Goulue, using the parasol she was carrying to indicate Dany.

"She is my new dresser," answered Jane.

La Goulue flashed the other dancer a triumphant smile. "I'm glad you think so, but Joseph thinks otherwise. I saw you come in with her; and while you were doubtless filling her head with lies and slanders about me, I went to Joseph's office and arranged for her to be *my* dresser."

"I'm sure I can help both of you into your dresses," said Dany.

"I am the star of the Moulin Rouge," said La Goulue. "I do not share my makeup, my clothes, or my dresser with supporting players."

"As if any of them could fit into your clothes anyway," said Jane Avril.

"This is the little girl who was with Henri last night," replied La Goulue. "He told me that he would make me the centerpiece of his new poster, as befits the star. Ask her if you don't believe me."

"He has also told me that he is still growing as an artist," Jane shot back. "When he has gotten all of his mistakes out of his system painting you and Nini, I may allow him to paint me again." A nasty smile spread across Jane's face. "Of course, he may run out of paint by the time he finishes your belly and your thighs."

Dany thought that La Goulue might take a swing at Jane Avril, or perhaps stab her with her parasol; but instead she threw back her head and laughed.

"So you are friends after all," said Dany, relieved. "For a moment there I doubted it."

"We are not friends," said La Goulue, "but when you are the star, you can afford not to hold a grudge."

"Everybody says that you are both stars," said Dany diplomatically.

"We are, for the moment," said Jane. "But I will continue to shine long after La Goulue has eaten and drunk herself into the grave."

"At least I will be a happy, well-fed corpse," said La Goulue.

"If not a clean one," said Jane Avril, wrinkling her nose. "When was the last time you bathed?"

"I bathe regularly once a month," shot back La Goulue. "All the parts that show." She turned to Dany. "It is not healthy to bathe too often. Too much water can damage the skin."

"Too much dirt and dried sweat can damage it even more," said Jane.

"Such airs!" La Goulue laughed. "To listen to her, you'd think she comes from royalty."

"Perhaps not royalty," said Jane Avril, "but my father was a honest merchant."

"Your father sold fruit out of a cart up and down the Seine," La Goulue corrected her.

"At least I know who my father is!" snapped Jane.

"A lot of good it did you," said La Goulue with a shrug. She winked at Dany. "Fathers are a greatly overrated commodity."

"I think I shall go and have a little chat with the esteemed

M. Oller," said Jane Avril, walking to the doorway and back into the corridor.

"He'll listen very politely and then tell her that you are my dresser," said La Goulue. "He knows better than to upset a star. Have you a name, girl?"

"Dany."

"Dany. A nice name. And I am Louise—but you must only call me that in this room. Out there"—she waved a hand in the direction of the dance floor—"I am La Goulue."

"Doesn't the name bother you?"

"Why should it? Nini has lovely thighs, and I am a glutton—for food, for money, and for love."

"I meant no offense," said Dany.

"Do I look offended?" said La Goulue with a smile. "I think we are going to be great friends, Dany. Perhaps in a few weeks I will even start teaching you to dance the can-can."

"Would you?" asked Dany excitedly. "I'd give anything to become a dancer at the Moulin Rouge!"

"Don't say that where anyone can hear you," said La Goulue. "There are altogether too many men who will take you at your word, and you would be surprised at how elastic a word *anything* can be." She looked at a clock on the wall. "Four-thirty. I'd better get to work."

Dany looked puzzled. "But there's no one here. The doorman told me that the club doesn't open until seven."

"That's the fun part of the job," said La Goulue. "The work takes place right here, right now. Help me out of this dress."

She turned her back, and Dany began the dress. Finally La Goulue stepped out of it, and stood there, hands on hips, wearing a camisole, a whalebone corset, and long white pantaloons.

"Loosen the stays a bit," she instructed, and Dany did her bidding.

Finally the dancer began bending over and touching her toes, right foot first, then left.

After a few minutes she lowered herself to the floor and began a number of stretching exercises.

"Do you do this every night?" asked Dany, fascinated.

"Every night," said La Goulue.

"Did you even when . . . I mean . . . ?"

"When I was younger and thinner?" said La Goulue with a chuckle. "Yes. You are what—twelve or thirteen years old, maybe even younger? Your body is limber. You have probably never broken a bone or pulled a muscle. But believe me, Dany, if every woman who dances at the Moulin Rouge didn't do stretching and warm-up exercises, half of the dancers wouldn't be able to get up after they did their first split."

"I didn't know that," said Dany. "You make it look so easy."

"You see," continued La Goulue, stretching her legs farther and farther apart, "there's more to being a star than meets the eye. I cannot be La Goulue only for the hour or two each night that I dance and flirt with the customers. I must be La Goulue whenever a man is around, or an audience, or the public at large. I can be Louise Weber only in this dressing room, or in my bedroom—and then only when I do not have a gentleman companion."

"But you must *want* to be La Goulue, or you wouldn't work so hard to be her," said Dany.

"Of course I do," answered the woman. "What is Louise Weber?

A pudgy woman who can barely read or write, who knows nothing of art or music, who came from nothing and will someday return to it. Why wouldn't Louise Weber do everything within her power to be La Goulue?"

"Maybe you won't return to nothing," said Dany.

"A dancer's life is not that long, Dany. Even if you can keep your body from breaking down, the public is very fickle. Next year they will fall in love with another dancer and will forget all about you. Much better to be poor Henri, whose work and reputation improves as he gets older, whose paintings will please people even after his death, when no one will be able to tell you who La Goulue was."

"Then why do you call him 'poor Henri'?" asked Dany.

La Goulue sighed. "Look at the man. It was as if God said, 'I will make you a great painter, but you must pay Me a tribute, and the tribute I demand is your legs.'" She shook her head sadly. "Did he tell you about his parents?"

"He said they live in Toulouse."

"So they do. His father refuses to see him. He feels that he has produced a freak and doesn't care to be reminded of it. His mother loves him dearly and wants only to protect him, to keep him hidden from the public view forever on their estate." She paused. "One thing I will grant him is his courage. He came here to get away from one parent who loathed him and another who loved him too much, and he does not hide. He visits all the clubs and bars, and he paints every day. More to the point, he paints *us*."

"You mean the dancers of the Moulin Rouge?" said Dany.

"I mean the people of Montmartre," answered La Goulue.

"Others use us, or are entertained by us, or take advantage of us. Only Henri lives with us and captures us on canvas. He takes from us, it is true, especially from the women—but he gives back even more than he takes." She studied Dany curiously. "What is your business with him?"

"I don't understand."

"I know his taste," said La Goulue. "You are too young to be his new lover."

"I most certainly am *not* his lover!" said Dany heatedly.

"Do not be offended. He has numbered among his lovers many of the most beautiful women in Montmartre." La Goulue smiled. "He found out very early on that the women of Montmartre are not offended by the sight of his legs, that we regularly see far worse things." She paused. "But if you are not his lover, what are you doing with him?"

"I helped him home two nights ago when he passed out on the street in Pigalle, and he got me this job to thank me." Dany decided not to mention that she was doubling for La Goulue in the preliminary sketches for the poster.

"Are you living with him?"

"He lets me sleep there," answered Dany. "But when I receive my salary, I will find a room of my own."

"Don't."

"I beg your pardon?"

"I will teach you to dance, but it is not much of a life unless you can become La Goulue; and there is only one of me, no matter what Jane Avril thinks. Most of the girls are gone by the time they are twenty. But if you can get Henri to teach you to paint, why, you can work until you die."

"I have been told that most painters die hungry," replied Dany.

"But they live a long time," said La Goulue. "Most canc-an dancers die young and hungry. I will keep my promise and teach you to dance, but you might consider that."

"I will," promised Dany.

CHAPTER SIX

A Model in Montmartre

When Dany woke up Henri was already working at his easel.

"Welcome to the world," he said when he saw her walk out of the bedroom.

"What time is it?" she asked.

"Almost one in the afternoon."

"You should not have let me sleep so long."

"I got home at three this morning and painted for another hour. You were not yet here by the time I went to bed. You are a growing girl; you need your sleep."

"La Goulue decided to do an extra dance for some of the customers, and then M. Oller told me to help clean the tables and the floors."

"He is certainly getting his two francs' worth from you," commented Henri dryly. "What does he have you doing? I never saw you, and I was there past midnight."

"Until the club closes for the night I am La Goulue's dresser."

"You have my sympathy. She is also a growing girl—just not in the same direction."

"She is very nice."

"You are not a rival—yet." He stared at her. "Well?"

"Well what?"

"Did you ask her, and did she agree?"

"I don't know what you mean."

"Did you ask her to teach you to dance the can-can, and did she agree?"

"Yes," answered Dany, surprised that Henri had guessed. Then, hesitantly, awkwardly she went on, "She suggested . . . well, she thought, that is . . . that perhaps you—"

"That I should teach you to paint?"

Dany nodded. "But you have done so much for me already."

"Nonsense," replied Henri. "That's the first intelligent thing she's said since I've known her."

"She says that most dancers die young and poor, and that there can be only one La Goulue."

"But there can be many Toulouse-Lautrecs?" he said, arching an eyebrow.

"I do not think she meant it that way," said Dany.

"You're probably right," agreed Henri. "She's not subtle enough."

"So will you?"

"Will I what?"

"Teach me to paint."

"A job *and* an education," he said, amused. "You put a higher value on my life than *I* do."

"If you don't, that's all right too," continued Dany. "What I really want is to be a dancer at the Moulin Rouge."

"It's no life for someone like you," said Henri. "If the alternative to teaching you is to watch you double your weight, eat everything in sight, and kiss every man who cannot fight you off, I shall teach you to paint."

"When do we start?" she asked. "I have three hours before I must report for work."

"We'll start right now," answered Henri. "You will be both my preliminary model and my pupil. Even when you are posing, I will explain what I am doing, and you will try your best to remember it."

"That seems fair."

"Would you like some breakfast first?" he asked. "I can have the concierge bring it up."

She shook her head. "No. M. Oller let me bring home some food from the kitchen. I ate it before I left the bedroom." Suddenly she looked distressed. "I should have offered to share it with you. It was very thoughtless of me. I am sorry, Henri."

"That's quite all right. I cannot face food this early in the day."

"For many people the day is half over," she noted.

"I am not many people," he replied. "I had a friend who died last year, a man who studied under the same master as I did. His name was Vincent van Gogh, and someday I think he will be acknowledged as a fine artist. He could paint a landscape, and in it the sun seemed so bright that it could burn you. Somehow you knew that if you stared at it without blinking you would go blind." He paused. "I have never painted the sun."

"Why not?"

"Vincent lived for mornings and sunlight. I am a creature of the evening, and so are my subjects."

"Why do you not paint landscapes?"

"Land is just land. It is people who are all different, and I paint the ones I find most fascinating."

"If you were in England, you would paint Queen Victoria?"

"Royalty holds no interest for me," he said. "If I were in England I would go directly to Whitechapel, the area that the notorious Jack the Ripper terrorized three years ago, and paint the faces I saw there."

"And probably the bodies," she added, staring at some of the nudes that lined the studio.

"They say that the eyes are the windows to the soul," said Henri. "Sometimes they are. But sometimes it is the body that is the window to the soul—if not the soul of the model, then of the artist."

"They just look like naked women to me."

"But you are looking at the finished products," said Henri. "Trust me, only an artist of exceptional imagination could make La Goulue look beautiful with her clothes off." Suddenly he smiled. "But don't tell her I said so."

"I will keep your secret," replied Dany, fighting back an answering smile. "She wouldn't believe it anyway."

"Perhaps she would be right," he admitted. "I made her a star, but thousands of people have seen her now, and she remains a star. The public has spoken." Another smile. "I knew there was a reason royalty never wanted to give the masses the vote."

"We should begin my lesson if I am to learn anything before I leave for work," said Dany.

"Five minutes more or less won't make much difference," said Henri. "Why, it might take you an entire week to become as good as I am."

"When you are all through teasing me, tell me what you want me to do," she said without rancor.

"I apologize, guardian angel," said Henri, suddenly serious. "I have been teased so often in my life that I tend to tease everyone I meet before they can tease me first. It is what that doctor of the mind in Vienna—Freud, I think his name is—calls a defense mechanism."

"I know your teasing is not mean-hearted," replied Dany.

"I hope you do. Now, stand over there," he said, indicating a spot on the floor about ten feet away.

She walked over. "Here?"

"Yes."

"What should I do now? I was allowed to watch the dancers when they worked, and I think I can hold my leg up next to my head the way Jane Avril does, with my toes pointing at the ceiling."

"You'll fall over."

"I can try."

"No," he said firmly. "And that is *not* teasing. Don't forget—you are La Goulue, not Jane Avril, and La Goulue does not hold her leg up like that."

"She did it when she was doing her exercises."

"That was doubtless without her corset and her high-heeled dancing shoes. Let me be the artist and *you* concentrate on being the model and doing what I tell you to do."

"Yes, Henri."

"Now, turn your back to me."

"You are going to paint La Goulue's back?" she asked. "That will not make people want to see her."

"Oh, I don't know. Once they know her, I suspect most of them want desperately to see her back."

"You are joking again."

"You noticed," he replied. "Now turn to your right, very slowly."

Dany did as she was instructed.

"Stop!"

She froze.

"Now turn again, even more slowly. . . . Good . . . Now stop." He began drawing furiously with his soft-leaded pencil. After a moment he looked up. "All right, Dany. You can relax."

"May I see what you've done?"

"Very little, but yes, take a look at it."

"It is very odd," she said, staring at the sketch he had just rendered. "I have my back to you, but somehow I can see my face, and it doesn't look like someone has twisted my head around and broken my neck."

"I'll work out the details later—what step she's doing, how much of her face you can see, because this strikes me as a little too much—but the princple is there."

"Could you explain the principle to me?"

"I want to show people that this is a dance hall and not a presidium stage, that it is huge, even for a Montmartre club. So there will be people at the back of the poster watching her, but if she were performing just for them, then her back *would* be all the poster could show and that would hardly attract patrons."

"Just as I said," commented Dany.

"On the other hand, if she faced the front of the poster, it would look posed, and it would also look like there was a section of the club, where the men and women in the background are standing, that she ignored, that never got to see her face."

"Ah!" she exclaimed. "I never thought of that!"

"So I will capture her as she is turning," he continued. "Her pantaloons will be so shocking to the average viewer that as long as I show them prominently, no one will notice that she faces neither the viewers of the dance in the painting nor the viewers of the poster. But it will make an impression on their minds nonetheless. They will say not only that this is a lovely and exotic woman doing a dance that is forbidden on most of the Continent, but that she spins around and plays to her *entire* audience rather than just one segment of it."

"And that in turn will convince them that wherever they are in the Moulin Rouge, they will be able to see the show," concluded Dany.

"You see?" said Henri. "You're learning already."

"What would you like me to do now?" she asked happily.

"Nothing. But when you go to the club this afternoon, see if you can get La Goulue to show you a few simple steps. Pretend you are wearing a belt right *here*"—he indicated a spot about an inch above her navel—"and remember that I don't want any steps that will have your toes above that point."

"Why not? All the can-can dancers kick their feet higher than their heads."

"This is a commercial poster, not a photograph. She will be wearing a full skirt; and if she kicks her foot above her head, as even the pudgy La Goulue can do, the skirt will rise and spread to accommodate the motion, and that in turn will cover most of what I plan to paint in the background."

"I never knew there were so many things to consider when you paint a picture," said Dany.

"I haven't even started painting," said Henri with a smile. "Before I do, I must decide not only upon the colors I need, but what type of paints I plan to use, how to mix the colors, whether to paint on paper or canvas, whether to fill in the entire painting with color or leave much of it untouched as the Japanese do. . . ."

"Why would you leave it untouched?"

"To draw your attention to what I *do* paint. You'd have to be a very strange observer to concentrate on blank space rather than the figure in the foreground."

"Did your friend Vincent leave blank spaces?"

"No."

"But if he was your friend . . ."

"It is all right to disagree with a friend," said Henri. "Besides, think of how dull the world would be if everyone looked like Jane Avril, beautiful as she is, or painted like me, talented as I am."

"I never thought of it that way," she admitted.

"You are very young," he replied gently. "There are many new thoughts waiting for you to discover them."

"Growing up sounds exciting when you say it that way."

"It all depends on who you are."

"You sound like you preferred being a little boy," observed Dany.

"I did," said Henri, "until I broke my thighs."

"But if you hadn't broken them, perhaps you would not have become a painter."

He shrugged. "Perhaps."

"*I* will be a painter and a dancer."

"Then instead of dying young and destitute, you will die young and talented and destitute."

"You are teasing again."

"I hope I am," he said. "Anyway, learn those steps. And while you are stuffing La Goulue into her dress, I will work on my latest portrait of Yvette Guilbert so that you do not miss any portion of the work I do on the poster."

"I saw one of your paintings of her on a poster that is hanging behind the bar at the Moulin Rouge."

"And what do you remember most about it?" Henri asked sharply.

"Her long black gloves."

A satisfied smile crossed his face. "I *knew* it!"

"You wanted me to remember the gloves?"

"The Moulin Rouge is a club that hires many beautiful women; and when there is that much beauty in one place, you must find ways to make each women stand out. With Yvette it is those black gloves that go up past her elbows. Whenever anyone sees a woman with those gloves, they will know it is Yvette if she is at the club—or if they see her elsewhere, it will remind them of her." He paused. "With Jane Avril, each time I paint her I give her a larger and more eye-catching hat."

"And what do you do to make La Goulue memorable?" asked Dany.

"You mean, besides taking forty pounds off her?" he replied with a smile. "She is the star, so she is always at the center of each poster,

just as she will be in this poster. Now, I know you are going to say
that every subject is in the center of the painting, and that is true,
but I never paint La Goulue alone. She is always surrounded—by
adoring men, admiring women, other dancers—so you *know* that she
is the star."

"And how will you paint me when you finally do my portrait?"
asked Dany.

"With a halo of course," answered Henri.

"You are teasing."

"Probably," he said seriously. "I have painted many things, but
never innocence. I may not know how to go about it."

She was silent for a long moment. "Henri?" she said at last.

"Yes?"

"I have a favor to ask."

"Then you should ask it immediately," he said, "so if I say no we
have time to make up and be friends again before you go to the club."

"Those francs you would not let me return to you," she said.
"May I spend them on a new dress? People stare at me with pity in
their eyes when I walk around the club in this dress, which I have
worn for as long as I can remember."

"They are your francs, to spend on anything you wish."

"Thank you, Henri. I think I will leave now and buy a dress on the
way to work."

She walked to the door.

"*Wait!*" he said sharply.

"Yes, Henri?"

He reached into a pocket and pulled out a ten-franc note. "You are my apprentice now, and your appearance is a reflection on me. Buy two dresses; and when one is being washed you can wear the other." He stared at her. "As for what you're wearing. . . well, I don't know any artist who can't always use more rags."

She took the note. "You are a very good man, Henri."

"I am a very good artist," he replied. "I am a rather mediocre man."

"You really must get out of this habit," she said.

"What habit?"

"You told me before how you tease others first. But you also tease yourself first. It is not necessary, Henri, for I will never tease you."

"Somehow I know you won't," replied Henri. He stared at her thoughtfully. "I think you are right, Dany. Others have mocked me all my life, so I insult myself before anyone else can. It is a habit I will try to break."

"I hope so," she said, opening the door. "I must go now. I promise to learn the steps so we can work on the poster tomorrow."

"Learn *only* the steps," he said, as she left and closed the door behind her. "That halo is very becoming," he continued, speaking to the empty studio. "I would miss it very much if you should misplace it at the Moulin Rouge."

CHAPTER SEVEN

A Shadow in Montmartre

Dany bought two dresses, one a light green, one a muted red. She folded the red one neatly, wrapped her tattered old dress around it to protect it, and wore the green one to the Moulin Rouge.

This time when she approached the door, Pierre greeted her amiably, tipped his hat to her, and stepped aside to let her pass by. As she was approaching the dressing room, she bumped into Joseph Oller.

"Good afternoon, Mademoiselle Angel," he said with an exaggerated bow. "How did your first day of employment go?"

"I enjoyed it," she replied. "Thank you once again for hiring me."

"You should thank your patron, M. Lautrec," answered Oller. "He has never before asked me for a favor." Suddenly he smiled. "I rather suspect he would have beaten me with his cane if I had refused."

"In front of everybody?" asked Dany, wide-eyed.

"Being the center of attention has never bothered our Henri." Oller laughed. "I understand that Louise has appropriated you as her dresser. Is this satisfactory to you?"

"Yes."

"Then everything is fine," he said. "I hope you will stay with us, Mademoiselle Angel. I have never had a dancer named Angel before." He studied her with an expert eye. "Another year or two, another inch or two, a little rounder here and there . . ."

"The delivery is late!" cried a distressed baritone voice from the direction of the bar. "We have only six bottles of absinthe!"

"Duty calls," said Oller with an apologetic smile. The sound of La Goulue's off-key humming came to their ears. "I think *your* duty calls too, Angel."

He went off to the bar, and Dany continued walking to the dressing room.

"Ah, there you are!" said La Goulue. "What a pretty dress! It looks new."

"I bought it earlier this afternoon," said Dany, turning around and showing it off.

"Be sure to wear an apron when you clean up later. That material will show dirt and spills."

"Yes, Mademoiselle."

"And speaking of dresses, take the ones I wore last night to M. Oller and tell him to have someone wash them."

"Yes, Mademoiselle."

"Good! Now help me out of my clothes," said La Goulue. "It is stretching time again."

Dany helped the dancer out of her dress, then stood behind her and loosened her stays.

"I wonder if I could ask a favor, Mademoiselle," she said hesitantly.

"Only your second day on the job and already you want to borrow my money or my men?"

"Oh, no, Mademoiselle!" exclaimed Dany. "I would never do that!"

"All right then," said La Goulue. "What particular favor did you want?"

"I wonder if you could show me some dance steps?" said Dany. "They must be very simple ones, because I do not think I can raise my foot above *here*"—she indicated her belt—"without falling down."

"Ah!" said La Goulue. "So you want to show off for some young man!"

Dany smiled without answering. She didn't want to lie, but Henri had warned her not to let La Goulue know that she was the dancer's stand-in for the preliminary sketching, and she decided there was a difference between lying and remaining silent (or if there wasn't, there *should* be).

"Wait until I have finished my stretching exercises, and I will show you some steps that will have him panting with passion," promised La Goulue.

"Thank you, Mademoiselle," said Dany sincerely. "I am in your debt."

"And someday when I am old and poor and you are the star of the Moulin Rouge, I shall collect on it," replied La Goulue with amiable insincerity.

Jane Avril entered as La Goulue was stretching. She offered a friendly greeting to Dany and a contemptuous sniff to her rival as she walked to her makeup table.

"Good afternoon, Mademoiselle Avril," replied Dany. "You look very lovely today."

"What has Henri been giving you to drink?" grunted La Goulue from the floor.

"Do not fret, *ma cheri*," said Jane to La Goulue. "We shall all join forces and pull you back onto your feet before the show begins."

"I'm sure M. Oller will appreciate that," shot back La Goulue. "It will be the first honest work you've given him since he hired you."

Jane Avril got out of her dress, hung it up, and also began stretching.

"I wonder where all the other dancers are?" said Dany.

"Oh, they'll wander in about five o'clock or so," said La Goulue.

"Or later," added Jane Avril.

"I find it strange that only the two biggest stars should show up early every day."

"Why do you think we *are* the biggest stars?" said Jane. "It is because we work the hardest."

"That's true," agreed La Goulue. "But my friend Dany misspoke. She meant the biggest star and the most notorious supporting dancer."

"It's the truth," said Jane Avril to Dany. "By the third show we *all* have to support her or she couldn't make it through to the end."

"Enjoy your dreams of future glory while you can," said La Goulue. "But when I finally retire, I think I will turn over the star's position to Dany here."

Jane Avril turned to Dany. "So you think you would like to be a dancer?"

"It looks exciting," said Dany.

"It *is* exciting," replied Jane. "And never more so than when you

are dancing next to La Goulue. You never know when she might col-
lapse from exhaustion and shatter your foot beyond all repair."

"Thank you for the suggestion," said La Goulue. "I shall seriously consider that the next time we are kicking side by side." She got to
her feet, grabbed a towel, and began dabbing at the beads of perspira-
tion that had appeared on her face, neck, and shoulders. "Well, Dany,
if I am to teach you, I suppose I'd better do it before the dressing
room becomes too crowded."

"You are really teaching her to dance?" asked Jane Avril.

"Just a few steps to amuse her boyfriend," answered La Goulue.

"If you really want to learn how to dance for a man, you should
come to someone who knows how," said Jane, straightening up and
walking over.

"She did," said La Goulue.

"Do not be afraid to tell her that she is past her prime, Dany,"
said Jane.

"I like you both," said Dany, clearly distressed. "Please do not
make me choose."

"Now you have upset her," said La Goulue. "Come, Dany. We
will *both* teach you, and you can tell your children, when you finally
have them, that you learned from the two greatest dancers in France."

"Perhaps in the world," chimed in Jane Avril.

"I thought you didn't like each other," said Dany, confused.

"What has that got to do with anything?" said La Goulue with a
laugh.

And for the next twenty minutes, they schooled Dany in the steps
that Henri had wanted her to learn. When Nini-le-Belle-en-Cuisse

arrived, they stopped, and Dany returned to her job of helping La Goulue into her stockings, dress, hat, and shoes.

When the show began and the girls raced out to perform the cancan, Dany remained in the dressing room, practicing the few steps she had learned until she was sure she could remember and perform them.

At the end of the final show, the women traipsed back into the room, and Dany began helping La Goulue out of her outfit.

"Did you hear the applause tonight?" said one of the younger girls. "That was the loudest it's ever been."

"Montmartre is becoming more popular every day," said Yvette Guilbert. "When M. Lautrec finally delivers his new poster, it will be more popular still."

"Long live Montmartre!" cried another girl.

"Where did Montmartre get its name?" Dany asked La Goulue.

"It is on the Butte, which is the highest spot in Paris," answered the dancer. "That's where the *Mont* comes from. Montmartre means 'Mount of Mercury.' You see, a Roman temple of Mercury once stood at the top of the Butte—"

"Rubbish!" said Jane Avril.

"Are you calling M. Oller a liar?" demanded La Goulue. "For he is the one who told me."

"He is not a liar, but he is wrong. M. Zidler told me that it means Mount of Martyrs and is named for St. Denis, the first bishop of Paris, who was tortured to death by the Romans."

"So the Romans had a temple here, and they tortured people?" asked Dany.

"But they make great macaroni," said La Goulue, which got a laugh from all the women.

After another hour all the women had left and Dany helped collect the dirty linens and wipe down the tables. Finally her chores were finished, and she went out through the front door of the club.

As she walked she became aware of a tall, shadowy shape following her. She increased her pace. The shadow began walking faster. She turned into an alley. It followed her. Now thoroughly frightened, she turned onto the rue Ravignon, sidestepped an emaciated dog that was growling and gnawing on the remains of a very small kitten, almost tripped over a body that was lying half on the sidewalk and half in the street, then took a left at the rue de la Mire, the shortest street in Montmartre. It quickly dead-ended on rue Lepic; and as she hurried down rue Lepic, avoiding the prostitutes and drunks who wandered up and down the street, she dared a quick look back. Now she could see his general outline: he was a tall thin man, well over six feet in height, as nimble as a stalking tiger, clad all in black.

She stifled a scream and broke into a run, not slowing down until she reached the door of 21 rue Caulaincourt. She raced up the stairs, flung open the door to the studio, entered, and slammed the door shut behind her.

"Henri!" she cried.

The artist had fallen asleep before the half-finished portrait of Yvette Guilbert. An empty bottle of cognac lay on the floor next to his stool. He awoke with a start, blinking his eyes very rapidly as he tried to focus them.

"What is it?" he asked groggily.

"How do I lock the door?"

He stood up and began rummaging through his pockets. "I know I had a key when I came home," he mumbled.

"Hurry, Henri!"

"Ah, here it is." He held it out to her. She grabbed it, rushed to the door, and locked it.

"Don't lose the key or we will never get out of here," he said, staring at her owlishly.

"A man followed me all the way from the club!"

Henri tried to concentrate. "A man? All that way? What did you do to encourage him?"

"You're drunk!"

"Of course I'm drunk. That is how I meet guardian angels on the streets of Montmartre."

She brushed by him, walked to the window, and peered out, but it was too dark to see if the tall black-clad man was there.

"Try to pay attention!" said Dany. "Whoever followed me knows where we live now!"

"Everyone knows where I live," he said with a drunken smile. "I am the famous Henri . . . Henri . . . ." He seemed to be trying to remember the rest of his name. "Well, I'm pretty damned important, whoever I am." He stared at her as if suddenly aware she was standing next to him. "So a man followed you from the club?"

"Yes."

"I'm insulted." He reached out clumsily and grabbed her arm. "I am only half a man, but then you are not yet a woman. I should certainly be man enough for you."

"Let me go, Henri!" said Dany.

"I feed you, I house you, I even found work for you—I should get something in return. Why must you save yourself only for whole men?"

"You stink of cognac!"

"Certainly I stink of cognac!" he slurred. "Do you think I could muster the courage to approach a woman, even a baby like you, if I wasn't drunk?" He pulled her closer and began running his hands over her. "Kiss me, and then tell me that the sight of me doesn't sicken you."

She tried to break away again, couldn't, and finally leaned forward and kissed him on the cheek. "The sight of you has never sickened me, Henri," she said.

His eyes focused for just a moment, and she thought she saw a tear roll down from one of them. "You lie exceptionally well," he mumbled. "Just for a second there I could almost believe it."

And with that, he passed out and fell unconscious to the floor.

CHAPTER EIGHT

A Drawing in Montmartre

Dany awoke to the small of coffee. She sat up, rubbed her eyes, then climbed out of bed and walked into the studio.

"You are awake," she said.

"Of course I'm awake," answered Henri, refusing to meet her gaze.

"I thought you would sleep all the way through until nightfall."

"Why would you think that?"

"You were so drunk last night, you couldn't even remember your name. And you grabbed me and wanted to—"

"It must have been *very* good cognac," he interrupted with a clumsy attempt at levity.

"If you keep drinking you will kill yourself."

"We must all die," answered Henri. "Very few of us are privileged to determine the method by which it will happen."

"You make a joke of it," she said severely, "but there is nothing funny about what you are doing to your body—and what you tried to do to mine."

"I cannot believe I am being lectured to by a child," he remarked with amusement. Suddenly the half smile left his face. "I recall almost nothing about last night," he added uncomfortably, still refusing to meet her gaze. "As for what I am doing to my body, that is nothing compared to what God has already done to it."

"But you are a great artist, and it would be wrong to rob the world of your talent."

"Now, *that* is perhaps the one argument I cannot refute," said Henri. "You are going to be quite a woman when you grow up, young Dany."

"Despite last night, I would rather grow up in a world that included you than one that didn't," she said.

"Maybe you will take my place when you are grown up," he suggested. Then he smiled. "Or are you intent upon taking La Goulue's?"

"You are teasing me again."

"Yes, I am," he admitted, "because I am ashamed of my behavior. The behavior," he continued wryly, "that I almost do not remember. I think in exchange for putting up with such abuse from such a freak—"

"You may be a drunk," she interrupted, "but you are not a freak."

"In exchange for putting up with such abuse," he repeated, "you deserve another lesson from the master."

"You mean we're going to work on the painting?"

"In an hour," he said. "But for now I am going to teach you the rudiments of drawing. We might as well find out if you will become the Toulouse-Lautrec of the new century."

He sat her down next to him, gave her a sketch pad and a piece of charcoal, and offered her some rudimentary instructions for the next forty-five minutes as she tried her best to follow his suggestions.

"They don't look like people," she said unhappily, fixing a critical eye on the figures she'd drawn.

"They're a very good beginning," replied Henri. "No one learns everything in a day, or a week, or a month. But you have made a nice start. Just remember that to be true to your art, you must paint your subjects not as a camera might see them, but as *you* see them. Sometimes the two are very similar, but more often they are not."

"I will remember, Henri," she promised.

"Good," he replied. "Now let us get to work before you must leave for the club."

"Where is your paint?" she asked.

"I won't be painting for a few days yet," he answered. "But even when I do, this is not a work that is to be framed and displayed. It is just a guideline for me when I create the poster." He turned to her. "Did you learn the dance steps as I requested?"

"Yes," she said. "La Goulue and Jane Avril both worked with me."

"Let me see the steps."

"I don't have fancy pantaloons or petticoats," she said apologetically.

"We will imagine them."

"All right," she said. "I hope you don't mind, but I find it easier if I hum the melody as I dance."

"I don't mind at all," said Henri.

Dany began humming to herself and then executed five very simple steps.

"Very good," said Henri. "I see a future in which you are a great artist by day and a great dancer by night. In both cases I shall be very sorry to lose you," he added sadly. Then he smiled again. "Perhaps I should just keep you totally ignorant and dependent upon me."

"No more teasing."

"All right, no more teasing." He took the sketchbook she'd been using and turned to a fresh page. "Let me see the fourth step you did, please."

"Are you sure?" she said. "I cannot hold that position long enough for you to draw it."

"The fourth step," he repeated.

She held her leg out straight ahead of her and began turning. After a few seconds she had to put her foot down on the ground to retain her balance.

"Again. And try to hold absolutely still once your leg is extended."

She performed the step again and held the pose for less than two seconds.

"Once more."

"But once I start turning, I must finish or I have to put my foot down."

"Just do as I ask."

After he had her repeat the step eight more times, he told her to sit down and relax.

"I hope you're not going to use that," she said. "I felt so awkward doing it."

"It won't look awkward in the painting."

"Why didn't you choose one of the more graceful steps?" asked Dany. "One where I wasn't falling over?"

"Because that step shows *motion*," answered Henri. "If a young, limber girl such as you can't hold that pose, believe me, La Goulue for all her experience couldn't hold it either; and it will be apparent in the painting. And that will mean that I've captured a single instant of time and that if you were there to watch her for the next few instants, she would finish spinning around."

He held the sketch he had done of Dany in his left hand and began transferring it, in considerably more detail and very bold lines, onto the easel as he spoke. Dany walked over to observe just as he leaned forward and drew a blond braid piled atop the figure's head. "The bosom and hips will come later," he explained. "But this makes her La Goulue rather than a much prettier dancer named Dany."

"Yes, that is how she wears her hair when she dances," said Dany. "I helped pin it in place." She studied the figure. "It is as if she is frozen in the middle of a kick."

"And since no one can hold that pose, the observer will imagine the rest of the spin and the kick," said Henri.

"Why do you use such a thick outline?" asked Dany. "It makes her look . . . I am not sure."

"Study her," he said, "and tell me why I use bold lines on my figures."

Dany stared at the drawing. "It makes her stand out," she said after a moment.

"That is right. This is where I differed with my late friend Vincent. He saw such beauty in landscapes, whereas for me nothing exists but the figure. The landscape should be merely an accessory. And of course when you are painting La Goulue, her landscape is the bar, the tables, and indeed the patrons."

"It makes sense when you explain it that way."

"Good," he said. "It never made sense to Vincent."

"How else will you make her stand out?"

He smiled. "How do you think?"

"You're not going to paint her with her clothes off?" she asked suddenly. "Not in front of all those customers!"

He laughed. "No, I am not. Not that it would bother her in the slightest."

Dany studied the paper again. "Perhaps some other dancers?" she suggested at last.

"What about them?"

"Maybe you should put them in the picture."

"They are very colorfully dressed, most of them are younger and prettier than La Goulue, and all of them are thinner," he answered. "They would draw your eye away from her."

She stared at the scene that was slowly taking shape. "I do not know, Henri. I am not a painter."

"You are not a painter *yet*," he corrected her.

"If there are secrets to making her stand out that I cannot see, then probably I will never be one."

"There are secrets to everything," he replied. "Do you think you could learn all the steps and then go out and dance the can-can in the Moulin Rouge?"

"Well, I know there are stretching exercises. . . ."

"There are dead spots on the floor that you want to avoid. There are girls who do not kick as high, and you will want to dance next to them to make your own kicks look more impressive. There are shoes that will ease the pounding your feet take. There are corsets that are made for such dancing. There are places on the dance floor where the lighting will make you look better or worse. There are ways to throw yourself into the air and land in a split that will not rip all your muscles away from your bones. There are—"

"All right," she said irritably. "It is clear that I know nothing about anything."

"That is not so," he answered. "But however much you think you know about something, there is always more to be learned. I will learn more about painting every day until I die."

"I am sorry I lost my temper, Henri," said Dany. "I just feel very stupid, and I am tired of feeling stupid. I have felt stupid my whole life."

"If you want stupid, try to converse with Nini on art, or Yvette on literature, or La Goulue on anything other than La Goulue," he said with a smile.

She looked at the picture again. "I still do not see how you can draw more attention to La Goulue."

"Let us make a puzzle of it," suggested Henri. "Let us assume that I will paint La Goulue as well as she *can* be painted. If I do that, then you are right about one thing: there is nothing else I can do to her to make her stand out even more." He paused. "But. . . ."

"But?" she repeated, puzzled.

"If I cannot make her brighter, prettier, bolder, or more interesting, what is my alternative?"

She frowned in puzzlement. "To make everything else *less* interesting?"

"Well, that is not precisely the way I would have worded it," he replied with a chuckle, "but you are in essence quite correct. I must do nothing to the rest of the picture that will distract from her."

"You have made a good start, if she is the only dancer," said Dany.

"True. But it is only a start. I have worked on various techniques that we will apply to this painting. Look around the studio, not just at the portraits of the dancers and the prostitutes, but even of the circus performers. Take your time, and when you have finished, tell me what it is that you don't see."

"That I *don't* see?" she repeated.

He nodded.

"You're saying that there is something that *should* be in each painting, but isn't there?"

"That's right."

"And whatever it is, it is missing from all of them?"

"Yes. Now find it while I do a little work on Yvette's portrait."

Dany began at the farthest wall, studying the nudes, the dancers, the singers, the elegantly clad patrons, the circus clowns, trying to determine what was missing. She was staring at an early painting of Jane Avril when she realized that her shadow was making the colors appear muted, and she moved to her right to allow the sun to bring out the full richness of the colors.

And then it hit her.

"I know!" she cried triumphantly. "I know what is missing!"

"Would you care to share that knowledge with me?" asked Henri, looking up from the portrait.

"Shadows!" she said. "There is not a single shadow in any painting in the room!"

"You are a fast learner," he said. "A properly rendered shadow will frequently take up more of the painting than the subject herself—and who wants to look at a shadow? I can change the flesh tones to reflect the light that falls on my subjects, but why in the world would I waste all that space showing their shadows on a wall or a floor?"

"So if there is no shadow, it will not distract you from La Goulue!"

"Right. Shadows are often elongated, or foreshortened, and if a shadow isn't an exact duplicate of the person casting it, it just naturally has to attract the attention because it is an unfamiliar shape." He pointed to his imported woodblock prints. "I learned that from the Japanese. Bold lines, bold colors, and no shadows."

"So that is how you will do it."

"That is one of the ways," answered Henri. "But there are others as well. Tell me, Dany, what is the most interesting thing about a human being?"

"I know what *you* think it is," she said disapprovingly.

"Let me rephrase that. What is the most interesting thing about a fully clothed human being of either sex?"

"The face."

"That is correct," answered Henri. "If you want to take attention away from a woman who is dancing for an audience, what would you do?"

"Draw interesting faces."

"And conversely, if you wanted to keep the attention focused on the dancer, what would you do?"

She frowned. "Draw blank faces?"

"You mean without eyes and noses and mouths?" he asked.

"I guess."

"Think about it, Dany. If someone created a bunch of blank faces, wouldn't they be the first things you looked at because they were so unusual?"

She nodded her head. "Yes."

"Then what else can we do?"

"Shadows?" she suggested, then made a face. "But you never draw shadows."

"True," he said. "But what is *like* a face that is entirely in shadow?"

"A silhouette!"

"That's right." He pointed to the large semicircle, the first thing he had drawn. "These will become some of the patrons of the Moulin Rouge; and if I show them all in silhouette, the club will seem just as crowded, but nothing in that crowd will take the viewer's attention away from La Goulue."

"There's a lot more to painting than you would think," said Dany.

"You just have to consider the result you want and almost work backward," said Henri. "Take La Goulue, for instance. One of her favorite tricks is to kick the hats off the patrons. It's a crowd-pleaser. Everyone loves it. It's one of the things for which she is most famous. But if I were to paint it . . . ."

". . . you would have to show the patron's face looking surprised, and you would show the hat in flight, and both would draw attention from La Goulue!" she concluded.

"Correct. It would make an amusing poster, but I'm advertising the club, not the patrons."

He began outlining a row of men in the background, men destined to become silhouettes.

"I don't know how you can do that so fast," said Dany in awed tones.

"Speed has nothing to do with quality," he said. "But while what I just drew would function well in a work of art, it will not do for a poster. Can you tell me why?"

She studied the row of patrons.

"They look fine to me."

"Apply the same principle you used with the shadows. Look at that line of patrons and tell me what you *don't* see."

"Oh! Of course! There are no women."

"Right. Now, the male customers outnumber the women; but while this poster will be a work of art, it must first and foremost be a work of *commercial* art, which is to say, it must make the Moulin Rouge seem inviting to *everyone*. Every healthy Frenchman wants to watch La Goulue and Jane Avril and the others dance the can-can, but the same is not true of every Frenchwoman, so we must show them that women *do* attend the show and enjoy themselves."

Henri glanced at his pocket watch.

"Is it time for me to go to work?" asked Dany.

"Soon," he replied. "We will not have time to lay out the entire picture today, but we can do one more thing: we can show how large the dance floor is."

"I know how to do that," volunteered Dany. "You make the silhouettes in the background much smaller than La Goulue."

"That is one way, yes."

"But the large man you are going to show on the right . . ." she said. "If you are not going to show his feet, people will not know if he is on the dance floor or standing well back from the floor, behind some of the tables."

"I shall consider that tomorrow," said Henri. "But for now there is another method we can use that has nothing to do with the man who will be in the front or the silhouettes at the back."

She frowned and stared at the picture. "But you don't have any other figures."

"True."

"Then what else can you do to show the size of the floor?"

He smiled. "Watch."

He took his soft-leaded pencil and drew a number of straight lines from the bottom of the picture to the row of patrons. The lines were wider apart at the bottom; and as they moved up the picture, they began converging at some unseen spot behind the patrons.

"The floorboards," he explained. "A dozen or so lines, and suddenly the floor is enormous."

"It is so difficult when you first ask about it, and then so simple when you do it!"

"Well, it's not *that* simple. You have to know exactly what effect you want and how to achieve it."

She began walking to the door, then turned and came back to him.

"May I borrow the sketchbook, and perhaps some charcoal or a pencil?" she asked. "Maybe I can make some drawings while the women are dancing."

He picked up the sketchbook and a pencil, and handed them to her. "Remember to bring back the book," he said. "I'd like to see what you draw, what interests you."

"Be honest with me, Henri, and no teasing," said Dany. "Do you really think someday I could become an artist?"

"It's difficult to judge based on a single hour," he replied, "but if a drunken cripple can become a great artist, then why not a healthy guardian angel?"

She walked to the door. "Promise you won't work on the picture until I come back."

"I probably won't work on anything," he said.

She sighed wearily. "You're going to get drunk again, aren't you?"

"Not again—*still*. Intoxication is my natural state, as sobriety is yours."

"I wish I knew why," she said, opening the door.

"I have many reasons," he said. As the door closed, a look of infinite sadness crossed his face. "And now I have another: that I won't live to see what kind of woman you grow up to be."

CHAPTER NINE

A Tavern in Montmartre

Jane Avril was already at the club when Dany arrived.

"Good afternoon, Mademoiselle Avril," said Dany.

"Good afternoon, Dany. Have you been practicing those steps you learned?"

"A bit," answered Dany. "I am afraid I am not very good at them."

"You will improve," said Jane. "That puts you one step ahead of La Goulue."

"Do you really dislike her so much?" asked Dany.

Jane Avril looked surprised. "I do not dislike her at all. I just object to the fact that she is considered the star of the show. In another year I will have enough money to start my own club, and there will be no doubt who is the star of *that* show." Suddenly she smiled. "If my club puts the Moulin Rouge out of business, you can always come and work for me."

"That is very generous of you," said Dany noncommittally.

Joseph Oller entered the room. "I do not mean to disturb you," he said. "I am looking for Yvette. We have purchased a new song that I would like her to perform tonight."

"She hasn't arrived yet," replied Jane Avril. "Only your two best dancers are here."

He stared at Dany and smiled. "So Mademoiselle Angel is to become a dancer?"

"Why not?" said Jane Avril. "She is already prettier than La Goulue."

"I will keep an eye on you, young Angel," he promised, and walked off in search of his singer.

"Could I really be a dancer?" asked Dany.

"If *la grosse vache* can, anyone can."

"Which do you love more, the dancing or the fame?"

"There are days when my knees hurt, when my muscles beg for relief—but there is never a day when I am tired of being famous," said Jane Avril. "Does that answer your question?"

"Yes, Mademoiselle," said Dany. "And now I have a favor to ask."

"Then ask it."

"I am not only learning to dance, but to draw. Do you mind if I try to draw a picture of your face? You don't even have to pose. I know what you look like, and I am just a beginner. It will not be a good drawing, but I will not do it at all if it might offend you."

"On the contrary, it flatters me," said Avril. "I haven't much time before I must begin stretching and getting into my costume, but I will pose for, shall we say, ten minutes?"

"That would be wonderful!" said Dany.

"Are you sure you want just my face?" asked Jane. "I have to take my clothes off anyway."

"Your face will be enough," replied Dany. "I am not as interested in naked women as M. Lautrec is."

Jane Avril laughed. "What do you expect? He is a man."

She sat on a wooden chair and struck a pose, and Dany began industriously trying to apply the minimal knowledge Henri had imparted to her earlier in the day. Dany had been working on the sketch for about five minutes when La Goulue entered the dressing room. She approached Dany, looked over her shoulder at the crude drawing, and nodded her approval.

"A vast improvement over the model," she said.

Jane Avril paid no attention to her, and never changed her pose.

"So our friend Henri is turning you into an artist," continued La Goulue. "Let me tell you, Dany, you will enjoy being a can-can dancer more. Every night is a party, and you will be surrounded by admiring men."

"I don't know if I will be any good at dancing *or* art," said Dany.

"Then you must keep practicing at both until you know," said Jane.

"That is correct," agreed La Goulue. "And while Henri teaches you to draw and paint, we will teach you how to dance."

"I have already told Joseph that she will become a dancer," said Jane. "I don't think we've ever had one quite this young, and I could see in his eyes that he was interested."

"Good. I will see him later and explain that she is being trained by the two greatest dancers in all France." La Goulue paused, suddenly realizing that she had complimented Jane Avril. "Myself and my closest competitor," she added lamely.

Jane Avril stood up. "I really must prepare now." She walked over to Dany. "May I see what you've done?"

"It's very poor," said Dany.

"Let me see anyway."

Dany showed her the sketch pad.

"And this is the first drawing you've ever done?" asked Avril.

"Yes."

"It shows promise." She handed the sketch pad back. "Now get out of your dress."

"Why?" asked Dany, startled.

"Because La Goulue and I are going to show you how to stretch and get your muscles ready to dance, and there's no reason to get your dress dirty."

"You're sure you don't mind?" asked Dany.

"You are our project now," said La Goulue. "Of course we don't mind."

Dany removed her dress and laid it carefully across a chair, then spent the next twenty minutes learning the dancers' basic warming-up exercises.

"How do you feel now?" asked Jane Avril as Dany got back into her dress. "A little stiff," she said. "Especially right here," she added, indicating her hamstrings.

"That's because you haven't done it before. In a few days it will make you feel better, not worse."

"Oh, I don't feel bad, Mademoiselle," Dany assured her. "Just stiff."

"Try dancing the can-can for half an hour *without* doing those stretches, and you'll know what stiff and sore really mean," La Goulue laughed. "Now help me into my dress, and then you may have the honor of drawing the fabulous La Goulue."

Dany spent the rest of the evening alternating between working on her sketch pad and helping La Goulue out of sweat-soaked dresses and into fresh ones. At one point Jane Avril asked for Dany's help buttoning up her dress, and La Goulue didn't even object.

At the end of the evening, Dany helped both women back into their street clothes (although, she decided, "street clothes" hardly described the expensive and elegant dresses they wore as they left the club). She spent another half hour making sure the makeup table was exactly the way La Goulue liked it, gathered the linens from the tables and cleaned the table tops, and then set out for Henri's studio.

Before she'd gone half a block, she realized that she was being followed again. She dared a single glance back, saw the same tall, black-clad figure she'd seen the previous night, and broke into a run. She didn't want to lead her pursuer to the studio, so she began racing blindly through Montmartre, turning into streets she had never seen before. Along the way she passed three men lying in the street, exactly as Henri had been on that first night; but she didn't dare stop. Twice she thought she had lost him, but both times she was mistaken.

A church! she thought. *There are always priests on duty. I'll be safe in a church!*

She looked around, panic-stricken. Where was the nearest church? She knew that St. Pierre de Montmartre was just off rue Norvins— but where was rue Norvins? She was all turned around.

The tall man appeared at the corner, and she stifled a scream and

ran in the opposite direction. Prostitutes and pimps, thieves and mug-
gers, all stared at her curiously but made no attempt to stop her or
help her.

*All right! It doesn't have to be a church! I'll be safe anywhere
there are people!*

The entire block was dark. It was close to three o'clock in the
morning, prime time for thieves and beggars, but all the normal people had gone to sleep.

She came to a cross street, turned onto it, and saw a light up ahead.

Where am I? She glanced at a street sign. *I wish I could read!*

She raced toward the light. At one point a cat hissed and jumped
into the shadow between buildings. Her legs felt heavier with each
step, and it was getting harder and harder to catch her breath.
She was afraid to look back, and finally she came to the source of
the light.

It was a crowded tavern with a darkened stage at the back. The
people inside weren't the types she would ever expect to see at the
Moulin Rouge. They were dirty, unkempt, unshaven, ungroomed. It
didn't matter. They couldn't be any worse than what was behind her.

She burst into the tavern, and suddenly every head turned to face
her. There were no friendly faces there, no welcoming smiles, just
curiosity that such a young girl had entered the place on her own.

She looked around the room. Every table was taken. There was a
bar off to the left; but she didn't want to get any closer to the men
who were standing there, some of them leering now and undressing
her with their eyes.

Finally a huge hulking man with a patch over one eye turned from the bar and approached her. He grinned, and Dany could see that his teeth were black and rotting away. She could smell him when he was still twelve feet away.

"A new angel of love," he said, "and I saw her first."

"Stay away from me," said Dany in a shaky voice.

"What will you do to me, child?" said the man with a coarse laugh. "Bite me in the knee?"

Dany backed away from him until she felt the front door behind her. She quickly stepped away from it in case the tall man was standing just outside, ready to grab her. But as she moved away from the door, she stepped closer to the one-eyed man.

He reached for her arm, laughing at her terror, and began running his other hand coarsely over her budding breasts.

Suddenly a female voice rang out: "Do not touch her!"

All eyes turned to the speaker, and Dany realized that it was Fabien, the woman she had met the same night she first encountered Henri.

"She is my sister," said Fabien. "She has come to give me a message."

"I don't believe you," growled the one-eyed man. "You never mentioned a sister before."

"I never talk to scum like you at all," said Fabien coldly. "If you do not leave her alone, you will have to answer to Jacques Nicot. Do you know what happens to his enemies?"

The man glared first at Fabien then at Dany. Finally he muttered an obscenity and returned to the bar. "Next time you will have no protector," he muttered bitterly.

"Come, sister," said Fabien, putting an arm around Dany. "We have much to discuss. Join me at my table."

She walked Dany to a small table in the corner. When they were seated, Fabien leaned forward and whispered, "Are you crazy? What are you doing here all by yourself?"

"A man was following me," said Dany, suddenly starting to shake. "I did not want to lead him to Henri's studio, so I ran."

"Henri?" repeated Fabien. "You are his mistress?"

"No!" said Dany angrily.

"Ah!" said Fabien knowingly. "He has thrown you out already, the drunken swine!"

Dany shook her head. "You do not understand. I work at the Moulin Rouge. M. Lautrec is letting me sleep in his studio until I can pay for a room."

"Who was following you?"

"I do not know. I came in here to escape from him."

"Do you not know where you are, Dany?"

"In a tavern."

"It is more than a tavern," said Fabien. "It is a cabaret, though no one is performing tonight."

"All right, it is a cabaret."

"You still don't understand," said Fabien. "You are in Au Lapin Agile."

Dany frowned. "I know that name from somewhere."

"You should. This is the notorious Cabaret of Assassins! You were safer on the street."

"What am I to do then?" asked Dany, almost in tears. "The man who was following me might still be out there."

"Stay here," said Fabien. "Do not leave this table."

She got up, walked over to another woman who was standing at the bar, and whispered something to her. The woman nodded and walked out the front door as Fabien returned to the table.

"I have sent for Jacques," she said. "He will be here in a few minutes and will escort both of us to my room."

"I don't know how to thank you, Fabien."

"That is easy," she replied. "Arrange for M. Lautrec to paint me. Perhaps he can make me as famous as La Goulue and Jane Avril."

"I promise I will speak to him about it."

"Tell him I consider clothes a nuisance. That may help him make up his mind."

"I will, Fabien."

"You are still trembling," noted Fabien. "Would you like some wine while we are waiting?"

Dany shook her head. "No, thank you."

"Who is this man who is following you?"

"I don't know," said Dany. "He has followed me two nights in a row." She paused. "Why? Why me? I am just a little girl. There are beautiful women all over Montmartre."

"If he follows us to my room, Jacques will get your answers for you," said Fabien. "Jacques is very good at cutting answers out of people who don't wish to give them."

"I don't want answers," said Dany. "I just want to be left alone."

"No harm will come to you tonight, Dany. You have my word on it."

Jacques Nicot entered Au Lapin Agile a moment later and walked straight to their table.

"Ah, the young lady from Pigalle!" he said, offering her a friend-ly smile. "We meet again."

"Suzette told you the situation?" asked Fabien.

He nodded. "Let's go."

Dany and Fabien got up and followed Jacques to the front of the tavern. He stepped outside first, looked down the street in both direc-tions, then held the door open for them.

"You will spend the night in my room," said Fabien. "There is no sense reporting this man to the police, not in Montmartre. But I am sure you will be safe in the daylight. As for tomorrow night . . ." She shrugged as if to say, To the residents of Montmartre tomorrow belongs to another century.

"Of course, if you were to work for me," said Jacques, "I would always know where you were, and could always protect you."

"She says she already has a job," said Fabien.

"Oh? Where?"

"At the Moulin Rouge."

Jacques looked at Dany. "You dance the cancan?"

"No," said Dany, "I am La Goulue's dresser. I help her into her costume, and I keep her makeup table, and I run errands for her, and I make sure her costumes are clean."

"La Goulue!" said Jacques. "I saw her once, almost a year ago. It was the only time I ever went to the Moulin Rouge." He smiled at the memory. "Do you know what she did? She kicked my hat right off my head—and I am not a small man!"

"That is one of her specialities," said Dany.

"When you go to work tomorrow, tell her that Jacques Nicot remembers her fondly."

"Does she know you?" asked Dany.

"No," he answered, "but I am sure she knows *of* me." They walked and talked, and within a few minutes they arrived at Fabien's building.

"Third floor, second room on the right," said Fabien. "It's not locked."

"Aren't you coming up too?" asked Dany.

Fabien smiled. "There is only one bed, and besides, my workday isn't over yet."

Dany shook hands with each of them in turn. "Thank you," she said. "I don't know what I would have done without you. How can I ever repay you?"

"I will tell you how," said Jacques.

"Yes?"

"Two years from tonight, I will come to the Moulin Rouge, and I will expect you to dance up to me and kick my hat off. That will be my reward."

Dany turned and entered the building before they could see the tears of gratitude roll down her cheeks.

"That was the first good deed I've done in ten years," said Jacques as he and Fabien walked back to Au Lapin Agile. "Who will pay me for it?"

"We will be rewarded," replied Fabien. "Our little friend is well-connected. She has been in Montmartre only a few days and already she works for La Goulue and lives with M. Lautrec." She paused.

"She is going to ask him to paint me, which will make me famous. And when she turns out to be another La Goulue or Jane Avril, doubtless she will remember who saved her life one dark night in Montmartre."

"True, true," said Jacques. "Two years from tonight she will kick my hat off, and three years from tonight she will be walking this very street in my employ."

"And when that comes to pass, don't forget my finder's fee," said Fabien. "She's going to be a lovely woman. It will be well worth it."

Suddenly he smiled. "You know, I think there may be something to this Good Samaritan business after all."

CHAPTER TEN

A Contortionist
in Montmartre

Henri was working on a painting of a clown when Dany entered his studio late the next morning.

"You did not come home from the Moulin Rouge last night," said the artist. "Where were you?"

"The tall man followed me again."

"You do not expect me to believe that you have been evading him for the past six or seven hours?"

"I spent the night in a friend's room."

"I didn't know you had any friends in Montmartre," said Henri.

"I have now—a woman named Fabien. I would like you to paint her."

"I have more work than I can handle."

"Henri, she saved me!" He sighed. "All right. Bring her around and I will see what I can do."

"It will have to be during the daytime," said Dany. "I do not think I am going to go out after dark again."

"You will lose your job," he pointed out.

"I can sleep at the Moulin Rouge."

"That's no way to live."

"Is drinking yourself into a stupor every night a better way?" she shot back.

"Touché," he said.

"Anyway, if I spend the night there, at least I know I'll be alive in the morning."

"I am truly sorry that you have had this experience," said Henri, his voice steeped with concern. "I will take steps to see that it doesn't happen again."

"*I'll* take the steps," she said adamantly. "I won't go out in the dark again."

"But you will still visit me during the day?"

"Of course."

"Good," he said. "I cannot teach you if you are not here." *And*, he thought, *I would desperately miss the only decent influence in my life. If you become an artist, we can continue to visit for years, whereas if you become a dancer, I may watch you at the club and I may paint you, but I'll never be close to you again. Our lives will head off in separate directions. I can't forbid you to dance, because that would just antagonize you, so I've got to make you more interested in painting.*

"What happened to the painting of Yvette Guilbert that you were working on?" she asked.

"It is done."

"So fast?"

He smiled. "When I drink, I drink, and when I paint, I paint." He paused. "Are you ready for another lesson? We'll spend an hour on it and then do some more work on the drawing of the Moulin Rouge."

"Yes," she said.

"First let me see what you drew last night."

She handed him the sketchbook.

"Not bad for a first try," he said. "These two are of La Goulue, of course, and this one with the higher cheekbones is clearly Jane Avril." He stared at another sketch. "But who is this?"

"That is my friend Fabien."

"Does she dance in the show?"

"No," answered Dany. "She is the one who gave me her room last night."

He continued studying the sketches. "Noses," he announced at last.

"Noses?"

"You have difficulty with noses. We'll work on that this morning."

They spent the next hour drawing noses—narrow ones, broad ones, long ones, short ones, upturned ones, hooked ones, bulbous ones. By the time they finished she was sick to death of noses, but she knew how to draw them.

"And now for the Moulin Rouge," announced Henri.

"When will you start painting it?"

He shrugged. "Today, tomorrow. It will take but a few hours."

"You can paint it that fast?" she asked, impressed.

"It will not be a painting for framing and hanging," he explained. "It is just a guideline for the poster, which will be the finished product." He removed the picture of the clown and put the one of the Moulin Rouge back on the easel. "First I must complete the foreground. Now, we know there will be a man on the right, and shortly I will draw him. But right now I must decide what to put in the left foreground."

"More people?" she asked.

He shook his head. "There are enough people. I need something to further suggest the interior of the Moulin Rouge."

"The bar?"

"No, that's not anywhere near the dance floor."

"What about the band?"

He considered it, then shook his head again. "It would just be more people." He closed his eyes.

"You're not going to pass out again?" she asked, wondering in what direction he might fall.

"No," he replied. "I am trying to visualize the club." He was absolutely motionless for a moment. Then he opened his eyes. "I have it!"

"What?"

"Those lovely overhead lamps that illuminate the dance floor," he said. He picked up his pencil and drew three circles in the lower left-hand portion of the picture. "Yes, that will work. They'll be yellow of course. It will give us some brightness, and will complement La Goulue's blond hair. They won't actually throw any light, and hence there will be no shadows, so I needn't worry about exactly how I place them."

He leaned forward and drew a few smaller circles above the silhouettes at the top of the painting. "See? The lights are all over, so they will lend a certain unity to the scene. Now all that remains is to sketch the man at the right and we will have the blueprint for our poster."

He reached out and created the broad outline of a thin man in a top hat. He began fleshing him out, adding a long neck, large hands, and formal dress. He had him arch his back, as if he had just completed a dance step.

Dany watched in fascination at first and then with a mounting sense of unease. Finally Henri began sketching in the man's facial features, ending with his prominent, jutting chin.

"That's *him*!" she cried so suddenly that Henri, startled, dropped his pencil.

"What are you talking about?"

"That is the man who has been following me the last two nights!" she said, pointing at the drawing. "I wasn't sure until you drew his chin, but now I am. If you know who he is, we must report him to the police!"

Henri chuckled in amusement. "*That* is the man who has been frightening you?"

"Yes!" she said, angered by his reaction. "Why are you laughing?"

"Don't you recognize him?"

"Yes—from the street!"

"That is Valentin-le-Désossé."

"Valentin the Boneless?"

"That's what they call him," said Henri. "He is a dancer and a contortionist. He works at the Moulin Rouge. You really never saw him there?"

"No."

"You have spent too much time watching La Goulue and Jane Avril. They may be the main attractions, but there are many others, including Valentin. He can stretch himself into the most remarkable positions."

"That is neither here nor there," said Dany. "We must report him."

"For following you?"

"Yes!" she snapped, frustrated. "Why can't you understand what I am saying to you?"

"I understand," he said, smiling.

"What is so funny?" she shouted.

"I *hired* him to follow you home, to make sure no harm befell you," said Henri, laughing again. "You have spent the past two nights running away from your protector!"

"I know why *you* didn't tell me," she said, still furious. "You were too drunk to remember. But why didn't *he* tell me? Why did he just follow me from the shadows and terrify me?"

"I have no idea," said Henri. "You will have to ask him at the club tonight."

"It was very thoughtless of you not to tell me, Henri," she said.

"I meant to," he said. "But then . . ."

"But then you would pass out on the floor again," she said.

"The drinking helps me to live with myself."

"It helps you to kill yourself."

"It makes the days bearable."

"How would you know?" she demanded. "You're never around at the end of one."

"I tried to do you a service!" he snapped. "I deserve better than this!"

"I fled for my life two nights in a row!" she yelled. "*I* deserve better than that! I am beginning to understand why you have driven away everyone you have ever loved!"

He stared at her with tortured eyes and made no reply.

Suddenly Dany felt her anger evaporate. "I am sorry, Henri," she said. "I did not mean to hurt you. You acted from the highest motives, protecting a girl who must walk through Montmartre in the middle of the night. I just wish . . ." She shrugged and stopped speaking.

"Everything you have said is true," said Henri at last. "I am thoughtless and self-centered, and I drive away the people I most wish to keep by me. I was too drunk to tell you that Valentin was there to protect you. I always mean to do well, and it always turns out like this. If it wasn't for my painting, I would be the most worthless man alive. Perhaps I am anyway." This was followed by a self-deprecating smile. "And that is another reason why I drink."

"I wish you wouldn't."

"And I wish for many things," he replied. "I won't enumerate them."

"You have a good heart, Henri," she said. "You do your best to hide it, but it is there. I just wish you didn't hate yourself so much."

He shifted uncomfortably, seemed about to say something, then changed his mind. Finally he spoke: "Shall we get back to work?"

"Yes, we might as well," answered Dany.

They both stared at the picture.

"Something is wrong," said Dany at last.

"I know. Can you see what it is?"

"La Goulue is not the star of the picture," said Dany. "Valentin is."

"That's right," agreed Henri. "And what shall we do about it?"

"Erase him?"

He shook his head. "That would put the picture out of balance."

"Then I don't know," said Dany.

"There is a way," said Henri. "And it is a way unique to the work of Henri Toulouse-Lautrec."

She studied the picture and shrugged helplessly.

"You do not see it?" he asked.

"No."

He smiled. "There are still some things at which I am competent," he said. "Observe."

He picked up a piece of charcoal and turned Valentin into a silhouette. "He is in the foreground," said Henri, "but if I refuse to draw shadows, then who is to tell me where I may or may not put my silhouettes?"

"I see!" said Dany. "Even though he is larger, and closer to the viewer, the eye travels immediately to La Goulue because she is the only figure who will be in color rather than silhouette."

"It is really quite simple, once you consider it." He smiled ruefully. "And it only took me a lifetime to think of it."

"And what will La Goulue wear?"

"Black stockings, of course, and white petticoats. Beyond that, I shall have to consider it."

"Then you are not going to paint right now?"

"I may not paint it at all," he said. "Or perhaps just the least bit of oils to go with the pencil and charcoal. As I said, this is really just a blueprint for the creation that is to follow—and I must complete it in the next few days, or I shall have to split your salary with Joseph again."

"Then you will go back to work on the clown?"

"Soon," he said. "I am very tired. I think I will rest first."

"You mean you will drink."

"That too."

"I will not stay and watch you," she said, walking to the door.

"I should apologize again," he said. "But why bother? I am what I am."

"You could choose not to be what you are."

"That choice was taken from me when I was fourteen years old."

"Many people suffer tragedies," said Dany. "They do not drown themselves in cognac."

"They cannot afford to," answered Henri. "They are not in line to inherit a fortune from fathers who cannot stand the sight of them."

"May I ask you a question, Henri?"

"A question?" He smiled ironically. "That might be a pleasant change."

"Do you become a better artist with each passing year?"

"I like to think I do."

"And do you live for your art?"

"You know I do."

"Then why kill yourself with drink before you are the best artist you can possibly be?"

He stared at her for a long moment. "Are you quite certain you have had no education?" he said at last. "You ask the most difficult questions."

"You didn't answer them."

"I will have to think about it." Another wry smile. "Of course, drinking helps me to think."

"Good-bye, Henri," said Dany. "I will be home after I am through working."

"Isn't it a little early to go to the club?" he asked.

"Isn't it a little early to start the day's drinking?" she shot back.

"I really do promise to consider your questions," he said as she walked out the door.

Dany headed straight to the Moulin Rouge, stopped by the kitchen for a cold piece of the previous evening's quiche, then went to the dressing room and spent the next two hours drawing sketches of everything she could see—chairs, vanities, costumes hanging on hooks. At four o'clock she walked out into the club and remained there for a half hour even though she knew La Goulue had already arrived.

Finally Valentin-le-Désossé entered the club. He was on his way to the men's dressing room when Dany walked over and stood in his way.

"Good afternoon, Mademoiselle Angel," he said, tipping his hat and bowing so low that she thought his chin might touch the floor. "We have not been formally introduced, but I am—"

"I know who you are," she said. "And I know you have followed me the last two nights."

"That is true," he said. "Though you led me a merry chase last night. What in the world were you doing in Au Lapin Agile?"

"Hiding from you."

He seemed genuinely surprised. "From *me*?"

"Yes."

"But I am your protector!"

"Nobody told me that. If you were there to protect me, why didn't you meet me at the door of the club when I left and walk me home?" He seemed puzzled. "M. Lautrec instructed me to follow you and make sure no harm came to you. He did not say to accompany you."

"You could have asked."

"But he was not at the Moulin Rouge the last two nights."

"You could have asked *me*."

"But *he* is my employer," said Valentin.

She saw the puzzled, hurt look in his eyes. He was not a very bright man, nor a very imaginative one. He was just following orders. Literally.

"Well, from now on I would prefer it if you would walk with me. That way people will think we're a couple and will be less likely to bother us."

"As you wish, Mademoiselle Angel."

"My name is Dany."

"That is not what M. Oller says, Mademoiselle Angel." She sighed. How could she get mad at a man who was just this side of simple?

"Anyway, I will look for you at the door when I am through working tonight."

"I will be there," promised Valentin.

"I hope M. Lautrec is paying you well for this service," said Dany.

"*Extremely* well, Mademoiselle Angel."

She couldn't resist finding out what he and Henri thought her safety was worth. "Is it many francs?" she asked.

"It is not francs at all, Mademoiselle," said Valentin.

"Oh?" she said, sure that Henri was taking advantage of the poor man. "Then how are you being paid?"

"He promised me that if I followed you and made sure you got home safely, he would put me in the poster of the Moulin Rouge," said Valentin happily. "I will be famous all over Paris!"

When she thought about it, she decided that he had made a pretty good bargain after all.

CHAPTER ELEVEN

A Poster in Montmartre

"I see you came home last night," observed Henri when Dany emerged from the bedroom in late morning.

"Yes."

"And have you made your peace with Valentin?"

"He walked me home," she said. "He is a very sweet man. Not a bright man, but a sweet man." Suddenly she smiled. "He walked on his hands for a whole block, just like Nini-le-Belle-en-Cuisse does at the club."

"I am glad you two are friends."

"We were never enemies," she said. "I just didn't know who he was, or why he would follow me at night."

"If you and I have made our peace, may I see your sketchbook?"

She handed it over to him, then watched his face apprehensively as he studied the pages.

"You're going to be very good someday," he said, returning the book to her after a few minutes. "Already I can see that you bring your own perceptions to the drawings. They are still crude, of course,

but less so every day." He paused. "You must always remain true
to that principle, Dany. You must paint things the way they appear to
you even if that is not the way they appear to everyone else. If you fail
to do that, you might just as well *be* a camera."

"I will remember, Henri."

"Good." He paused. "Well, today is the day."

"The day?"

"Today we will create the poster."

"So soon?"

"I am not yet twenty-eight years old, and already I have completed more than three hundred and fifty paintings and two thousand
drawings. I do not expect to live to a ripe old age, so I do not waste
my time once I sit down to work."

"You could, you know," she said. "Live to a ripe old age, I mean."

"Save the lectures for tomorrow," he replied. "Today we work."

"Yes, Henri."

"The first thing we must decide are the colors—not for this
drawing, but for the poster. I added some oils to the charcoal last
night, but it is still just a blueprint. But now I will choose the colors,
and you will write them down on a page of your sketchbook so that
I don't forget them when I prepare the lithograph." He paused.
"All we know so far is that the lamps and La Goulue's hair will be a
bright yellow."

"La Goulue has costumes of almost every color," offered Dany,
"so you can use any color you want."

"Lithography can handle hundreds of colors, but it is still an inex-
act science, and I prefer to use as few as possible." He paused. "But

because I use so few colors, it means that certain things that might be black in a painting will have a color in the poster." He pointed to La Goulue's legs. "Her stockings, for example. We will make them a russet red, and we will make the ribbon she wears around her neck the same color."

"But she has not worn dark red stockings since I started working at the Moulin Rouge."

Henri smiled. "I won't tell anyone if you won't."

She returned his smile. "It will be our secret. That is two colors—yellow and red. How many more will you use?"

"Probably just one . . . but that will be another of our secrets," he replied.

"I do not understand."

"You will. We will use red for her blouse, but instead of darkening it as we do with her stockings and her ribbon, we will lighten it with flake white until it becomes an orange-pink. The polka dots will be white, like her petticoats and pantaloons, but we will take that orange-pink of her blouse and use it on her lips as well." He smiled again. "She paints her lips so often, and with so many colors, who is to say that this isn't one of them?"

"So you are still using just two colors, red and yellow," said Dany. "I assume you will mix bits of black to darken the red, just as you mix bits of white to lighten it."

"That is correct. But we must do still more with the red. We must darken it again, but not quite the way we darkened it for La Goulue's stockings."

"Why?" she asked curiously.

"The silhouettes in the background can be black," answered Henri. "After all, they are the background. But Valentin is the largest figure in the picture."

"But you explained that you were making him a silhouette so the eye would be drawn to La Goulue," said Dany, confused.

"That's right. But this is a commercial poster, designed to make the Moulin Rouge seem bright and gay and fun filled. I cannot have the closest figure to the viewer, the biggest figure in the painting, be black, as if no light ever fell on him. We want La Goulue to be the brightest thing, of course—but we also want the viewers to know that this is a nightclub and a dance hall, not a theater where everyone sits like a statue in the dark and barely speaks above a whisper."

"So what will you do?" she asked.

"I will make him a single dark color, but I will hint at his facial features, his collar, and his arms. He will become not a silhouette but rather a semi-silhouette, and he will be a deep reddish brown rather than black."

"Maybe he won't be black, but he'll still be a dark color. Will it really make that much difference?"

"It will," Henri assured her.

"So that takes care of all the lamps, of La Goulue, of Valentin, and of all the spectators, with just two basic colors," she said. "What other colors will you use?"

He nodded. "Just one—the other primary."

"Blue?"

"Very good," said Henri.

"But what will be blue?"

"You'll see."

"And that's everything?" she asked.

"Not quite everything, but those are all the colors we'll need."

"What's left?"

"As I keep explaining, this is a poster, not a painting to hang in a museum," said Henri. "Don't you think we should tell the viewer what it is a poster *of*?"

"Oh!" she said, embarrassed. "I had quite forgotten."

"I will paint the words *Moulin Rouge* in red letters," he said. "In fact, I think I will paint them two or three times, so no one ever sees one of my posters without knowing what it depicts."

"And *still* no new colors," added Dany, impressed.

"None. I will leave some room beneath the club's name, and I will insert La Goulue's name there."

"She will like that."

"I will put it in black, so that it does not stand out as much as the words *Moulin Rouge*."

"She *won't* like that," said Dany.

"If she asks, I'll simply explain that red fades when exposed to sunlight and black doesn't."

"I didn't know that."

"I don't know it either," he said, flashing her another smile. "But it sounds good, doesn't it?"

She threw back her head and laughed. "When you are all through being an artist, I think perhaps you should become a politician."

"I do not lie enough to become one," he answered. "Now that I think about it, I do not even drink enough."

She looked at the poster-to-be again. "How will you darken the red to create the shades you need?"

He shrugged. "I'll use either burnt umber or dark sienna. It depends on what Charles has in stock."

"Who is Charles?"

"Charles Lorrilieux," answered Henri. "He manufactures inks. Just as I get my cognac at the Moulin Rouge, I always get my lithographic inks from Charles."

"You have forgotten something," said Dany.

"Oh?"

"The dance floor."

"That's what the blue is for."

"I've never seen a blue floor."

"And you won't see one in this poster," said Henri. "When I have finished with the basic colors, I'll use *crachis*."

"You'll *spit* on the poster?" she asked, surprised.

He chuckled in amusement. "No, I will not spit on the poster."

"But you just said—"

"It is the term for a lithographic technique," he explained. "Actually, the entire term is *grille à crachis*. I will make the floor and the area behind the onlookers yellow. Then I will hold an iron screen over the poster and scrape it with a stiff brush loaded with blue ink. The spatter will not be visible without a magnifying glass, but its effect will be to turn the yellow floor and background varying shades of green, depending on how much blue ink I use."

"Really?"

"That is how green is made—by combining yellow and blue."

"I didn't know that."

"There is no reason why you should. You have never painted

before."

"But if you buy all your inks from Charles, why not just buy green ink from him?"

"Because Charles is a businessman and not an artist. To him green is green," answered Henri. "But to me there are a thousand shades of green, and only one shade is right for any particular need. I prefer to make my own."

"And then you will be done—after you have made the brush spit on the poster?"

He smiled. "Then we will be done with that stage of the poster. After that I will go to the lithographer's, and we will prepare the poster for reproduction, probably using zinc. The lithographer recommends aluminum, but I have been unhappy with the results when I have tried it. We'll use a chemical treatment to fix the image on the printing surface; and finally, when I am satisfied with every detail, we will begin printing the poster. I'll examine the first few and then probably every twentieth one."

"It sounds mechanical, like printing a newspaper," said Dany. "Can't you leave it to the lithographer?"

"It is my name that will go on the poster—*here*." He pointed to a spot in the lower left-hand corner. "It is my name that will be seen in a thousand venues. If the colors are wrong, if the outlines are not as bold and strong as I intended, they will not blame the lithographer, whose identity they will never even know. It is *I* whose reputation will be enhanced or diminished by the poster; and since that is the case, I will see it through every stage of its creation."

"Does Charles use the same names for the colors of his inks that you use for your oils?"

"I haven't the slightest idea," answered Henri.

"But—"

"I tell him what colors I want and he supplies that. I have no interest in what he calls them. His job is to give me what I ask for, and my job is to pay for it."

She stood back and stared at the picture once more.

"The poster will make you the most famous man in Paris," she said at last. "And La Goulue will be the most famous woman." She sighed. "I wish I were older, so that it could be me in the poster."

"Perhaps in five more years you will be the star of the Moulin Rouge *and* the greatest painter in France," said Henri. "Then you can do your self-portrait as a can-can dancer and be the most famous woman in all Europe."

"You are teasing me again."

"True," he admitted. "But it is my fondest wish that someday that teasing becomes the truth."

Suddenly she frowned. "What time is it, Henri?"

"Not quite two o'clock."

"I must leave."

"Isn't it early to go to work?"

"La Goulue gave me some money to buy more of her favorite perfume," said Dany. "I will purchase it on my way to the club." She walked to the door, then stopped and turned to him. "May I tell her how good the poster will be and how famous you will make her?"

He nodded. "As long as you don't tell her what model is hiding beneath her image."

She smiled. "That, too, will be our secret," she promised.

CHAPTER TWELVE

A Morning in Montmartre

A week had passed.

The pop of a newly-opened champagne bottle woke Dany just before noon.

"Wake up, wake up!" chanted Henri in a sing-song voice. "You must not sleep away this beautiful day!"

She sat up in her bed and rubbed her eyes. "Please, Henri. I had to clean extra tables last night. I am very sleepy."

"You can sleep some other time! Come into the studio and have some champagne."

"In the morning?"

"There is no bad time for champagne."

"If I were to listen to you, there is no bad time for cognac, brandy, or absinthe either," she said grumpily. "I am going back to sleep."

"Not today!" he said happily. "Today we are celebrating!"

"What are you celebrating?" she said. "Have you found a new brand of cognac?"

"Has anyone ever told you that you are less than charming in the morning?"

"I think you just did," she muttered, finally getting to her feet and trudging into the studio. "All right, Henri," she continued, stifling a yawn. "What are we celebrating?"

"The Moulin Rouge."

"I don't have to celebrate the Moulin Rouge," she replied. "I work there."

"Not the club," said Henri. "The poster!"

"They printed it already?" she asked, suddenly alert.

"Yesterday," he said. "They printed four thousand copies, and posted them all over Paris."

"That's very nice, Henri, but you are acting like it's news. You knew they were going to do that."

He couldn't keep a smile off his face. "They had to print three thousand more this morning, and they are printing still more this afternoon."

"I do not understand," she said with a puzzled frown. "Why would they print so many more?"

"By this morning people had stolen three thousand of the posters to take home and hang in their houses!" he said. "Every store, every building, every business is asking for more posters. In twenty-four hours it has become the most popular poster in history!"

She emitted a happy shriek. "That is wonderful news for you, Henri!" she said.

"For *us*," he corrected her. "You were my assistant and my model, weren't you?"

"Yes, but no one will ever know that."

"You know it and I know it," he said. "And who else counts? Now have some champagne."

"Just one glass," she said. "I have to leave for work in a few hours."

"Not today, you don't," said Henri. "I have already sent word to Oller that you are to be my guest at the Moulin Rouge tonight. They are even now preparing pheasant under glass for the artist and the young lady who kept him sober long enough to complete the poster that is the talk of all Paris."

"Do you mean it, Henri," she asked, "or are you teasing me again?"

"I mean it."

"It will be wonderful!" she enthused. "We will eat dinner, and watch La Goulue, and then, while the dancers are resting, you and I will dance around the floor."

"I do not dance," said Henri.

"Neither do I," she said. "Except for a few can-can steps. We will teach each other, and everyone in the club will see that I am dancing with the greatest artist in the world!"

"*No!*"

She jumped, startled.

"I did not mean to yell," he said, trying to gain his composure. "Listen to me, Dany. I know how I appear to others. I am a freak, something to stare at in amusement or disgust. I will not add to people's amusement and disgust by stumbling around a dance floor."

"You are *not* a freak, Henri. And if you think otherwise, you are wrong."

"I know what I am."

"Everyone knows what you are, and what you are is a great artist. I have only heard one person ever call you a freak, and that person is Henri Toulouse-Lautrec."

"I am sorry I lost my temper with you, Dany," he said, suddenly contrite. "But I will not make a spectacle of myself. If you wish to dance, I will pair you with the most graceful and boneless partner anyone has ever had."

"But I don't want to dance with Valentin. He has talked to me the last eight nights as he walks me home, and he has yet to say anything interesting, whereas the only time you are not interesting is when you are drunk."

"Which is most of the time," he replied with a sardonic smile.

"Very well," she said. "This is your celebration, and if you choose not to dance, we will not dance. I will not speak of it again."

"Tonight you will have a more important function than dancing anyway," said Henri.

"Oh?"

"You must protect me from Jane Avril and the others. I seem to have made La Goulue the most famous woman in France."

"They will not want to harm you, Henri," she said with a smile. "They will offer you gold and diamonds beyond imagining to put them in your next poster."

He chuckled. "If that is all they offer, they are poor negotiators indeed."

"Perhaps you will paint my friend Fabien ahead of all of them. I have told her you agreed to see her, so I think she will come here to meet you one day soon."

"Possibly I have already sketched her," he said. "I have so many drawings . . ."

"She says you have not."

"Then I shall look forward to meeting her." He poured himself another glass of champagne.

"Maybe I shouldn't be the only one to limit my champagne this afternoon," said Dany.

"I am," said Henri. He held up his glass. "This is left over from the morning."

"When will I get to see the poster?"

"Right now, if you'd like," he said, indicating a rolled-up copy that leaned against the door. "I was out early today."

She walked over, picked it up, and tried to unroll it; but her arms were not long enough to hold it open, and it kept curling back up.

"Here," said Henri, getting up painfully and shuffling over to her. "Let me assist you." He helped her unroll it again and held the top against a wall. Then he reached into a pocket, pulled out a tack, attached one corner, and repeated the process three more times.

"You knew we were going to hang it on a wall," she said. "That's why you had the tacks in your pocket."

"True," he replied. "But it would have been presumptuous to have hung it before you even said you wanted to see it."

"You know I want to see it. And the man who created the most famous poster in the world is allowed to be a little presumptuous in his own studio." She stood back and studied the poster. "You were right."

"About what?"

"Everything. Not making Valentin a black silhouette. Not having the lamps throw shadows on the floor. Not having La Goulue standing still. Making the Moulin Rouge's name in brighter colors than hers. Everything." She paused. "I am so proud to have had something, however small, to do with it."

"I am glad you feel that way."

She stared at the poster for another minute, then turned to him. "I have never eaten pheasant under glass before. What do you do with the glass?"

"I'll give you a hint: you don't eat it."

"I know that—but I do not want to do the wrong thing, not with all the people I work with looking at me."

"Now you know how I feel about dancing," said Henri. "There's no need to worry. Just watch me and do what I do." Suddenly he smiled. "At least until I've had too much cognac and fall off my chair."

"Try not to do it before dinner, Henri," said Dany. "I will be very hungry by then."

"I shall put forth my best effort," he promised her.

"I have another question."

"About pheasant?"

"No," she said. "About stockings."

"They go on the legs."

She ignored his answer and continued: "Last night La Goulue told me she had bought six new pairs of silk stockings and told me to throw her old ones out. I threw out five pairs, but there was one pair that was undamaged, and I took it home with me. Do you think she would be upset if I were to wear the stockings tonight? If she sees them, she'll know they are hers."

"You will not wear someone else's stockings on the night of our greatest celebration," said Henri. He withdrew his wallet and handed her two francs.

"This should buy the best stockings in all Montmartre."

"I didn't mean for you to do that, Henri."

"If you had wanted me to, I probably wouldn't have done it," he replied. "Go now, in case it takes you a long time to make up your mind."

"Thank you, Henri," she said, walking out the door.

She went directly to a little shop she had passed on boulevard St. Germain, where, after looking at every sample in the shop, she bought a pair of bright red silk stockings. Then she crossed the street to the Marché Buci, the liveliest market in Montmartre, and used her change from the stockings to buy a pear, which she thought would hold her until dinner.

She spent the next hour wandering through the district, surprised at how safe and different Montmartre seemed in the daylight. She looked in store windows, imagining what it would be like to own some of the clothes she saw. She passed three posters of the Moulin Rouge, but when she retraced her steps on the way home, two of them were already gone.

When she entered the studio, Henri was lying on the floor. At first she thought he was dead, but then he groaned and she realized he was simply drunk again. He was too heavy for her to lift, so she went to the sink, filled a glass with water, carried it back, and threw the water in his face.

"I'll be all right," he muttered. "I just needed a little nap."

"How much champagne did you drink?" she demanded.

"I don't know. But I know one thing: it doesn't go well with absinthe."

"I will walk to the club and tell M. Oller to cancel our dinner, because you are in no condition to go."

"I'm going!" he yelled angrily, suddenly almost sober. "Tonight is my night to celebrate, to show them that the ugly little freak with the dwarf's legs did something all France can be proud of. I will not be denied my moment of triumph!"

He got clumsily to his feet, steadied himself against the easel before he could fall over again, and slowly focused his eyes. "Did you buy the dress?" he asked at last.

"The stockings."

"Whatever."

"Yes, Henri."

"Well, get into them. It's time for me to go to the club and take my bows."

"The club won't open for two or three more hours yet, Henri," said Dany.

"Then we will get dressed very slowly. Start now."

"No, Henri."

"Why not?" he demanded.

"I know you, Henri. You just want me out of the studio so you can drink some more."

He glared at her, but made no reply. Finally he pulled a charcoal out of his pocket and sat down at the easel. "Well, if you won't leave, you won't leave. Stand where I can see you. There's no sense wasting the whole afternoon."

"I would rather pose for you when you're sober," she said.

"And I would rather be six feet tall," he said. "We can't have everything we want. Now stand still."

She stood still.

CHAPTER THIRTEEN

A Celebration in Montmartre

She posed for almost two hours. By then it was starting to get dark and Henri was just about sober. They dressed in different rooms, and when they were ready they walked out onto the street, where Henri summoned a horse and buggy. They rode in luxury to the Moulin Rouge, and Pierre the doorman looked surprised when he saw who he was helping down from the painter's carriage.

They had just been escorted to their table when Joseph Oller rushed up. "Henri!" he said, throwing his arms around the artist. "You have not only created the most brilliant poster anyone has ever seen, but you have single-handedly created almost six thousand new thieves!"

"But each thief will know what club to come to when he goes out at night," answered Henri.

Oller laughed. "There will be no charge for you and Mademoiselle Angel tonight." He clapped his hands above his head. "Your attention, please!" he announced. "The Moulin Rouge is proud to have with us tonight the artist whose poster has taken all Paris by storm."

Suddenly there was a standing ovation, and the curtains on the walls were drawn back to display fifty framed posters.

Henri bowed awkwardly but happily and sat down. The next hour saw a steady procession of people—friends, strangers, dancers from the club—coming up to congratulate him. Henri insisted on having a drink with each and so was in no condition to eat his pheasant when it finally arrived.

Valentin approached the table, took off his top hat, and bowed low, bending almost in half at the waist.

"I want to thank you, M. Lautrec," he said. "Yesterday no one had ever heard of Valentin-le-Désossé. Today I am more famous than any man in Paris except yourself."

"It was my pleasure," slurred Henri.

"How can I thank you?"

"The young lady you have protected so admirably expressed an interest in dancing earlier today. Since I clearly cannot accommodate her, perhaps you will be my substitute."

"I should be honored." He held out his hand to Dany. "Mademoiselle Angel?"

Dany would have preferred to eat, but she didn't want to hurt Valentin's feelings, so she took his hand and accompanied him to the dance floor. They made an odd-looking couple, the tall lean Valentin and the small girl barely into her teens; but he was a thoughtful partner, and even though she did not know how to dance with a man, she was able to keep up with him.

When the band stopped playing and they returned to the table, they found La Goulue and Jane Avril sitting there, talking to Henri.

"Very graceful," he said, though Dany was sure he hadn't been watching.

"Thank you," she said. "But I really don't know how to dance."

"I thought these two lovely ladies were teaching you."

"That is the can-can, not dancing with a partner."

"Well, let me see what you have learned."

"Everybody will be watching," she said uncomfortably. "I'd rather not."

"This is my night," he said drunkenly. "You cannot refuse my request."

"Come," said La Goulue. "Jane and I will dance with you."

Jane Avril smiled. "And we will charge M. Oller extra for it."

Henri patted the glass that covered the pheasant. "View it as dancing for your supper."

"But—"

"I insist!"

She sighed. "All right, Henri, if I must."

"You must."

"Come on, Dany," said La Goulue. "It will be fun." She got up and began walking to the dance floor.

"I will go tell the band to play some Offenbach," said Jane Avril, heading toward the bandleader.

"I feel very awkward," said Dany. "I do not know that many steps."

"Just do the ones you know," said La Goulue. "No splits until you learn how. Besides, you haven't done any stretches."

"I didn't know he was going to make me dance."

"He will never create another poster like this," said La Goulue, "so he will never have another night like this. I suppose we can humor him this one time." She looked back at the table. "Doesn't he ever get tired of drinking? How can he create such beautiful work when he is so drunk he can't see straight?"

"I don't know," said Dany. "Every day when I come home he has passed out from too much cognac or absinthe; but before he passes out, he has always done more work in a few hours than most painters do in a week."

"He is going to die very young, you know," said La Goulue.

"I hope not," said Dany.

"We all hope not," said La Goulue. "But he is going to die very young."

Jane Avril rejoined them. "The music will start any moment."

"Already the people are giving us room," noted La Goulue. "It took them a while to notice that we are on the floor, but now they expect a show."

"Then we shall give it to them," said Jane Avril.

"I'm not capable," said Dany.

"We will just do the steps you know," said La Goulue.

"They will want you to do more."

"Then they can wait for the show to start."

The music began, and La Goulue and Jane Avril locked arms with Dany. Then they walked out to the center of the floor and began going through Dany's limited repertoire of steps. The audience seemed to sense that they were her mentors rather than her partners and cheered wildly every time Dany completed the simplest maneuver.

"This is *fun*!" said Dany a few minutes into the dance. "I can't imagine why I was so scared!"

"Well, she has the right attitude to be a Moulin Rouge dancer," Jane Avril said, laughing.

The tempo of the music increased.

"One last spin and we'll take our bows," said La Goulue. "Each in turn; and since I am the star, I will go last."

Jane Avril didn't argue. She stepped forward, held her left leg straight out, and whirled around a half-dozen times. Then, never losing the beat, she danced back to the other two and indicated that it was Dany's turn.

Dany held her leg out, not as high as Jane Avril, and slowly spun around, then did it again as the patrons applauded encouragingly. She noticed that Henri was on his feet, applauding.

"Faster!" he cried.

"Just once more, then stop," said La Goulue.

All right, Henri, thought Dany. *I've never spun three times in succession, but if that's what it takes to make you proud of me . . .*

She began her third spin and tried to go faster. Suddenly she thought she heard a gunshot, and then a woman screamed.

Oh, my God! Someone has been shot!

She realized that she was staring at the ceiling.

Was it me? Am I the one who was shot?

She became aware that La Goulue and Jane Avril were kneeling beside her, uttering soothing words that were somehow incomprehensible to her. Then Valentin lifted her and carried her off the dance floor.

"I'll bet you could have heard it snap all the way in the kitchen!" said La Goulue.

Suddenly Dany became aware of an excruciating pain in her right ankle.

"What happened?" she asked. "Who was shot?"

"No one, *ma cheri*," said Jane Avril, walking beside her and holding her hand as Valentin carried her to the dressing room. She smiled. "You just ended your spin a little too soon."

Before Dany passed out from the pain, she had only one question: "Is Henri mad at me for spoiling his celebration?"

CHAPTER FOURTEEN

A Decision in Montmartre

"Will she walk again?" asked Henri when the doctor had finished setting her broken ankle.

"Of course," answered the doctor. "She is young. She will heal."

"*I* was young," Henri said bitterly. "*I* never healed."

"Yes you did, M. Lautrec. You healed. Your problem was that you never grew."

"Is she in much pain?"

"Breaking an ankle is never painless," said the doctor. "And this wasn't a minor fracture. She shattered a bone. She'll have pieces of that ankle floating around down there for the rest of her life."

"But she *will* walk?"

The doctor nodded. "Yes, she'll walk. I told you that already. But I hope she had not planned to be a dancer, for dancing is something she will never do again. She will not need a cane, but she will probably always have a limp."

"It is my fault," said Henri miserably. "I am the one who urged her on."

"It is no one's fault, monsieur. Bones break." The doctor attempted a smile. "That is why we have doctors."

"You will send all your bills to me," said Henri.

"But M. Oller has already offered to—"

"You heard me," said Henri firmly. "Send them to me."

"Yes, M. Lautrec." The doctor walked to the door of the dressing room. "The girl is resting now. I am going out to the dance hall to have a drink and watch the show, which I have never seen." He smiled and shook his head in wonderment. "It is amazing the places one's profession takes one."

He left the room, and Joseph Oller entered.

"How is she, Henri?"

"She will always have a limp."

"It is bad luck," said Oller.

"It is more than bad luck," said Henri bitterly. "It is bad associations. She would be perfectly fine now if it hadn't been for me."

Oller was used to the artist's arrogance, but this was the first time he'd ever seen him riddled with guilt and self-loathing, and he was momentarily taken aback. "I've ordered a carriage to take her back to your studio," he said at last.

"*No!*"

"What is it, Henri?"

"I am the reason she broke her ankle," said the artist. "It is entirely my fault. I cannot face her."

"Be reasonable, Henri. She can't live *here*."

"I know." He walked to the door. "I have given the matter some thought. Wait here. I'll be back soon."

Oller sat down on a chair at La Goulue's dressing table and sighed deeply. It was such a shame that this had to happen tonight of all nights. Pierre the doorman had turned away almost five hundred people at the door; newspapers were begging for interviews with him, with La Goulue, even with Valentin. This should have been the happiest night of the Moulin Rouge's brief, three-year existence. Instead . . .

Henri returned almost an hour later.

"Well?" asked Oller.

"Everything is arranged."

"Would you care to confide in me," said Oller, "since you are my artist, Angel is my employee, and the accident took place in my club?"

"I have spoken to a friend. I believe you know his work—Edgar Degas."

"The one who paints the young ballerinas?" said Oller. "Yes, I know him."

"We used to have studios right next to each other a few blocks from here, and we became good friends."

"Don't tell me about Degas," said Oller irritably. "Tell me about Angel."

"There is an empty apartment in the building where Edgar lives. I have rented it. She will live there and study art with him. I have hired a nurse to stay with her while she is incapacitated."

"And Degas is doing this out of friendship?"

"I'm sure he would if I asked him to, but I didn't. I am paying for her rent, her food—she will take her meals with his family—and her lessons."

"And this arrangement, it will last until the cast is off her foot?"

"It will last until she is a grown woman."

"All the visits you will pay her will be hard on your legs," said Oller.

"I have no intention of visiting her," replied Henri.

"This is outrageous!" snapped Oller. "You can't do this to her, Henri!"

"I am doing it *for* her."

"You are doing it for Henri Toulouse-Lautrec and no one else!" said Oller angrily. "You will hurt her beyond measure if you refuse to see her. She is just a child. She will not know why you have rejected her. She will be sure she did something to offend you, and no one will be able to convince her otherwise."

"She will be much better off," said Henri uncomfortably, "and I have seen to it that she will have no financial concerns while she is growing up."

"Damn it! You cannot buy your way out of every situation you find unpleasant, Henri! Has it occurred to you that she may prefer your company to Edgar's? She doesn't even know him."

"It is not her choice," said the artist. He looked at Oller through tortured eyes. "I know what it means to damage a limb. I cannot face her again."

"So *she* must suffer for *your* feelings of guilt?" demanded Oller. "It was an accident. It could have happened to anyone."

"But it happened to someone who would never have danced if I hadn't gotten drunk and insisted upon it."

"This is ridiculous! She is part of the Moulin Rouge family, and she will always be welcomed there. Am I to warn you each time she is in attendance?"

"It would be considerate of you."

"You go to hell, Henri!" exploded Oller. "I refuse to be the only considerate man in this room!" He glared at the artist. "Maybe you should consider giving up drink rather than giving up your friendship."

A look of infinite sadness crossed the artist's face. "I wish I could, but . . ."

"But?"

"I could sooner run up the side of a mountain than overcome my weakness."

CHAPTER FIFTEEN

A Hospital in Montmartre

Ten years had passed.

They had been long, hard years for Henri. He had achieved a fame most people only imagine, but while his work was in greater demand than ever, his health had steadily deteriorated.

His drinking got worse with each passing year. By 1898 he had developed a persecution complex, convinced that the police were trying to kill him. The next year he went berserk in a brothel and was locked away in an asylum, where he remained for three months. By the dawn of the new century he was confined to a wheelchair; his painting had all but ceased, but his drinking hadn't.

In the spring of 1901 he suffered a cerebral hemorrhage, and as a result his legs were paralyzed. While recuperating in the hospital, he received an unexpected visitor.

"Good morning, Henri," said the pretty young woman. She carried in a large, thin package, almost three feet long, and leaned it against a wall. He stared at her, puzzled.

"Do I know you?"

"You did once," said the young woman.

He frowned. "You look familiar." A pause. "I knew a little girl with your features and coloring once, but that was many years ago."

"Ten years, to be exact."

"Then it *is* you!"

"Yes, Henri," said Dany. "It is."

"I am glad to see you looking so well."

"I am sorry to see you looking so poorly."

"I am dying," said Henri. "They will move me to Taussat in another month, but it will not help. I shall not see the end of summer."

"I know," she said. "That is why I am here."

"To gloat?" he asked without rancor.

"Of course not, Henri," said Dany. "I am here to say good-bye."

"You do not still hate me?"

"I never did."

"But your ankle . . ."

"You didn't break it, Henri. *I* did." She smiled. "I would probably never have been good enough to dance in the Moulin Rouge. You let me do it for one night. I will always be grateful for that." She paused. "For a while I thought I hated you."

"As well you should have. It was my fault."

She shook her head. "I do not know how such a great artist can know so little of the people he paints. I never blamed you for my ankle, Henri. I blamed you for turning your back on me, for sending me away and refusing to see me again."

"But I destroyed your career."

"I was a thirteen-year-old girl, Henri. I had no career. I had a friend and mentor, and he turned his back on me. And since I was only a little girl and I all but worshipped him, I did not understand that he too had weaknesses, even if they weren't the ones he complained of."

"So you do not hate me," he said, his voice echoing his relief.

"I tried to tell you."

He looked puzzled. "You did?"

"Twice I got up the courage to go to your studio and explain that I neither blamed nor hated you, but both times you were too drunk to recognize me. After that I stopped trying."

"All those years . . ." he said wistfully, then, "I am glad I could apologize to you before I die."

"Are you in much pain, Henri?"

"I have moved beyond pain," he replied. "We will speak no further of me. What are you doing now? I know you studied with Edgar for six years."

"Of course you know. You paid him." It was not a question.

"I forbade him to tell you that," said Henri angrily.

"He never told me. But I know *you*, Henri. You were always generous—with your money." She paused. "No more recriminations. In answer to your question, I have become an artist, as you always knew I would. I paint tourists' portraits along the Seine, and with the money I make I take more classes."

"I am sure you are a fine artist."

"I hope someday I will be." She paused. "I brought you a present."

He nodded toward the package. "One of your paintings?"

"A portrait." She began unwrapping it. "It is my farewell present to you."

She handed it to him, then limped to the door.

"It looks like me," he said, frowning. "But the proportions are wrong."

"Are they?"

"I thought I taught you to paint exactly what you see. When did I ever appear to be six feet tall with strong, straight legs?"

"Every time I ever looked at you, Henri," said Dany.

Then she was gone.

Toulouse-Lautrec's Life and Art

He should have spent his days on horseback and his evenings playing cards in private salons or at elegant parties. He should have known and mastered every popular form of dance, as well as the traditional ones. He might have sneaked off on rare occasions to watch the can-can dancers at the Moulin Rouge or perhaps even frequented a high-class brothel, but he would have made certain that no one ever knew of it.

That's what Henri Toulouse-Lautrec *should* have done. What he did was so much more interesting. And important.

Raised to be a member of the idle rich, he broke his thighs as a boy, and his legs never grew again. The rest of him grew at a normal rate, giving him a somewhat grotesque appearance when he reached adulthood; and it was this appearance that seems to have influenced almost every choice he made thereafter.

He chose not to be coddled in secrecy. He chose not to live far from prying eyes on a country estate. He chose not to hide from the public. An outcast by a fluke of fate, he chose to live among other outcasts, and to immortalize them with his art.

While others were painting landscapes and churches, Toulouse-Lautrec painted what *he* knew—and what he knew were women of the night, denizens of the dark streets and alleyways of Montmartre, nightclub dancers, circus performers, and the like. Now and then he would paint the rich and famous, but only when they came slumming to Montmartre.

He studied with Vincent van Gogh, he had a studio next door to Edgar Degas, he knew many of the important painters of the era; but he developed his own unique style, influenced more by the techniques of the Japanese woodblock print artists than by any of his contemporaries.

And he was prolific almost beyond belief. From the time he moved to Paris until he was too sick to work, a period of more than a dozen years, he averaged better than a painting a week and better than a drawing a day. Given how many days he was too drunk even to see the canvas or the sketch pad, that figure becomes even more remarkable.

Over the years his name and art have been most closely associated with the Moulin Rouge. (For what it's worth, John Huston's 1952 movie *Moulin Rouge*, starring Jose Ferrar as Toulouse-Lautrec, has an opening sequence of about ten or twelve minutes that is as true a representation of the Moulin Rouge of the early 1890s as you're ever likely to see. It's available on DVD.) Anyway, if the Moulin Rouge is known throughout the world more than a century after it first opened, all the credit goes to Toulouse-Lautrec.

Though he made a handsome living as an artist, he was most famous for his posters, and the art critics of his day tended to think of posters as "mere" commercial illustrations, hardly worthy of notice. When he died in 1901, his mother gathered most of his paintings, drawings, and prints and offered them in one huge package to museum after museum, with no takers. Finally, after twenty-one years of rejection, she offered them to the city of Albi, which not only accepted them, but built the Musée Toulouse-Lautrec to house them. Other family members who had inherited some of the artwork also donated it to the museum, which today holds more than one thousand pieces. The critics who snubbed Toulouse-Lautrec might be surprised (or dismayed) to know that the value of the collection is currently estimated to be well over two hundred million dollars.

His father couldn't look at him, and others teased him, and still more felt sorry for him, but posterity has made the little artist with the stunted legs nine feet tall.

A Timeline of Toulouse-Lautrec's Life

1864   Henri-Marie-Raymond de Toulouse-Lautrec-Monfa is born on November 24 in Albi, a city in the south of France.

1868   Henri's younger brother dies and his parents separate.

1878   In May Henri breaks his left thigh in a fall.

1879   In August Henri breaks his right thigh. Both of his legs stop growing. He never reaches a height of five feet.

1881   Henri decides to become an artist and moves to Paris.

1882   Henri studies briefly in the Bonnat studio, then moves to Ferdon Corman's studio in September. He befriends Vincent van Gogh.

1884   Henri moves to 19 rue Fontaine in Montmartre; meets Edgar Degas, whose studio is in the house next door; and develops a great admiration for his work.

1885   Henri begins frequenting Montmartre's cabarets and brothels, and the people he sees there start appearing in his work.

1887   Henri takes part in a collective exhibition in Toulouse in May under the assumed name of "Treclau," an anagram of "Lautrec," then exhibits with van Gogh in Paris. He begins to develop an interest in colored Japanese prints.

1889   The Moulin Rouge opens at 82 Boulevard de Clichy on October 5. Henri becomes a regular. He has a table reserved and displays his work there.

1890   Henri meets Jane Avril and creates a painting of the Moulin Rouge that owner Joseph Oller buys and hangs in the club.

1891   Henri make his first lithograph engravings and creates the Moulin Rouge poster that brings him overnight fame.

1893   Henri has his first large private exhibition. It is an enormous success. He now lives in a brothel that has been converted from a seventeenth-century palace. He creates his second most famous work, the poster for Jane Avril's show in the Jardin de Paris.

1895   Henri's drinking is seriously out of control, but he continues to produce numerous paintings and lithographs.

1896   He has a major private exhibition and refuses to sell one of his paintings to the king of Serbia, whom he drunkenly claims is nothing but a "pig farmer."

1897   Henri's productivity dwindles down to almost nothing, and he has an attack of delirium tremens.

1898   The drinking continues. He develops a persecution complex and believes he is being stalked by police who want to kill him.

1899   When Henri's not drunk, he's suffering from fits of depression. He goes berserk in a brothel on the rue des Moulins, and is confined to an insane asylum in February, where he remains for three months. The endless publicity surrounding his antics actually causes his work to rise dramatically in value.

1900   Henri stays reasonably sober until he has a huge fight with his family, who want him to have a guardian. He starts drinking heavily again and by midyear is so weak that he is confined to a wheelchair.

1901   By March Henri has suffered a cerebral hemorrage, and as a result his legs become paralyzed. He leaves Paris for the last time in mid July, suffers a stroke in Taussat, and is now paralyzed on one side. His mother takes him to Malromé, where he dies on September 9 at the age of thirty-six.

FOR MORE INFORMATION

Biography:

Toulouse-Lautrec: A Life, by Julie Bloch Frey (Phoenix Illustrated, 1995)

Study:

Toulouse-Lautrec and Montmartre, by Richard Thomson, Phillip Dennis Cate, and Mary Weaver Chapin (Princeton University Press, 2005)

Biography and art combined:

Toulouse-Lautrec in Paris, by Frank Maubert (Assouline, 2005)

Art:

Toulouse-Lautrec: The Theatre of Life, by Matthias Arnold (Taschen, 2000)

Toulouse-Lautrec: The Soul of Montmartre, by Reinhold Heller (Prestell, 1997)

Original art on display:

The greatest number of Toulouse-Lautrec's paintings reside at the Musée Henri de Toulouse-Lautrec in Albi, France.

Most major American and British museums display his paintings, usually on loan from France, from time to time.

Web sites:

There are dozens, probably hundreds, of sites with Toulouse-Lautrec's paintings. The three best to learn about him are:

http://colveyco.com/gallery-annex/reading/artists/lautrec.html

http://www.luxurytraveler.com/toulouse-lautrec.html

http://www.artelino.com/articles/toulouse_lautrec.asp

The Spirit Catchers:
An Encounter with Georgia O'Keeffe
by Kathleen Kudlinski

Like thousands of other Americans during the Great Depression, Parker Ray finds himself homeless and desperate. Now all signs—from his thirst-induced hallucinations to the inhospitable force of nature, Georgia O'Keeffe—tell him that something in the desert is out to get him.

"Kudlinski evokes the extremes of desert life, from desolation to sun-baked beauty, and then depicts the environment's mesmerizing effect on her characters . . . There are enough surprises to keep the pages turning . . . The notion of 'spirit' is woven effectively into a variety of contexts . . ." —*School Library Journal*

"Kudlinski succeeds amazingly at helping her readers look, really look, at the art of Georgia O'Keeffe."—Sam Sebasta, Ph.D., College of Education, University of Washington

". . . the plot takes off partly on the strength of Kudlinski's . . . portrait of O'Keeffe."—*Kirkus Reviews*

". . . the overwhelming feeling at the end is that the reader is 'inside the art, free to comment, and encouraged to experiment.' "—The Historical Novel Society

Hardcover ISBN: 0-8230-0408-2   Price: $15.95
Paperback ISBN: 0-8230-0412-0   Price: $6.99

Smoking Mirror:
An Encounter with Paul Gauguin
by Douglas Rees

The White Wolf killed his best friend. Now Joe Sloan seeks revenge. As he navigates the unknown territory of 1891 Tahiti and its people, he finds an unlikely ally in the French artist Paul Gauguin.

* A JUNIOR LIBRARY GUILD SELECTION *

"An intimate peek at Gauguin's creative process and the story behind the cover painting Matamoe with just enough action and native color to entice."
—*Kirkus Reviews*

"Like other titles in the new Art Encounters series, this weaves biographical facts about a famous artist into a compelling novel . . . . Rees has clearly done his research, and he admirably incorporates Gauguin's work and voice into a romantic coming-of-age story that asks compelling questions about how artists create and where their lives and art intersect. An afterword and a timeline of Gauguin's life will help readers separate fact from fiction."
—*Booklist*

" . . . fascinating, spellbinding, even educational."
—Mike Resnick, Hugo-award winning author of *Kirinyaga*

Hardcover ISBN: 0-8230-4863-2   Price: $15.95
Paperback ISBN: 0-8230-4864-0   Price: $6.99

Casa Azul:
An Encounter with Frida Kahlo
by Laban Carrick Hill

Maria and Victor journey in search of their mother through a Mexico City populated by godlike wrestlers—the mighty El Corazón and his nemesis El Diablo—a blind guitarist named Old Big Eyes, and a talking monkey. But a far more magical place exists: Casa Azul, the home of the painter Frida Kahlo.

". . . Hill's blend of realism, fantasy and Aztec myth nicely mirrors Kahlo's surreal juxtaposition of real and unreal in her lifelong attempt to paint her own reality. Magical realism from cover to cover." —*Kirkus Reviews*

"Like his subject's art, Laban Hill's encounter with Frida Kahlo is a richly imagined, seamless mixture of magic and reality that reveals, for readers, the larger truth of the artist's passionate life and work." —Michael Cart, editor, *Rush Hour*

"The book and the whole story are great. I felt like a kid reading every word on the page! I like the strains of magical realism coming through. The story has charm and reads like a thriller." —Margarita Aguilar, assistant curator, El Museo del Barrio

"Highly recommended to introduce the sophisticated young reader to this fascinating artist." —*Children's Literature*

Hardcover ISBN: 0-8230-4863-2   Price: $15.95

The Wedding:
An Encounter with Jan van Eyck
by Elizabeth M. Rees

In fifteenth-century Belgium, young Giovanna Cenami resists an arranged marriage in favor of true love. Who wouldn't choose a handsome and valiant youth over a seemingly dull merchant ten years her senior? Or is there more than meets the eye?

"... Rees, a painter herself, brings Jan van Eyck's vision to life in ways few could have imagined. Though set in 15th-century Europe, Giovanna's struggles seem both appropriate to her time and relevant to the struggles facing American teenagers." —Rochelle Ratner, executive editor, *American Book Review*

"A page-turning, lively historical YA romance plot spiced this a soupcon of star-crossed lovers .... Along the way, readers will encounter well-integrated, fascinating information on the period as well as the materials and techniques of the painting." —*Kirkus Reviews*

"A story as rich and textured as the painting that inspired it." —Ellen Steiber, author of *A Rumor of Gems*

"Elizabeth M. Rees has a true gift for bringing art and history vividly to life. Her story kept me up until the wee hours of the night, and I didn't want to leave the fifteenth-century when it was done!" —Terri Windling, six-time World Fantasy award-winning author of *The Wood Wife*

Hardcover ISBN: 0-8230-0407-4   Price: $15.95